A Treasury of Disney
Little Golden Books

22
BEST-LOVED DISNEY FAVORITES

gb GOLDEN PRESS • NEW YORK

Western Publishing Company, Inc.
Racine, Wisconsin

Contents

Snow White
AND THE SEVEN DWARFS

ONCE UPON A TIME, long, long ago, a lovely Queen sat by her window sewing. As she worked she thought, "If only I had a little daughter, how happy I would be."

Dreaming, she pricked her finger with her needle. Three drops of blood fell on the snow-white linen.

"How lovely my little girl would be if she had lips as red as blood, skin as white as snow, and hair as black as ebony," thought the Queen.

Some time later, a little daughter was born to the Queen, and she named the baby Snow

beautiful. She was jealous of all the lovely ladies of the kingdom, but most jealous of the lovely young Princess, Snow White.

Now the Queen's most prized possession was a magic mirror. Every day she asked it:

> *"Mirror, mirror on the wall,*
> *Who is the fairest of us all?"*

If the mirror replied that she was fairest in the land, all was well. But if another lady was named, the Queen flew into a furious rage and had her killed.

As the years passed, Snow White grew more and more beautiful, and her sweet nature made everyone love her—all but the Queen.

The Queen's chief fear was that Snow White might grow to be the fairest in the land. So she banished the Princess to the servants' quarters, made her dress in rags, and slave from early morning until late at night. But while she worked,

White. But the Queen was very ill. Holding her lovely child in her arms, she died.

When the lonely King married again, his new Queen was as heartless and cruel as she was

Snow White dreamed beautiful daydreams about a handsome Prince who would someday carry her off to his castle in the clouds. And day by day she grew still more beautiful.

At last came the day the Queen had been dreading.

"Mirror, mirror on the wall,
Who is the fairest of us all?"

she said. And the mirror replied:

"Her lips blood red, her hair like night,
Her skin like snow, her name—Snow White!"

The angry Queen hurried from the room and called her huntsman to her. "Take the Princess into the forest and bring me back her heart in this jeweled box," she said.

The huntsman bowed his head in grief. He had no choice but to obey the Queen's command.

OFF INTO THE FOREST went Snow White and the huntsman the next day. It was beautiful among the trees, and the Princess, not knowing what was in store for her, skipped along beside the huntsman, stopping to pick violets and singing a happy tune.

At last the huntsman, heartbroken, fell to his knees beside the Princess.

"I cannot kill you, Princess," he said, "even though it is the Queen's command. Run into the forest and hide, and never return to the castle."

Alone in the forest, Snow White wept with fright. But she was not really alone, she found. All the little woodland animals were her friends. Chattering happily, they led her to a new home.

It was a sweet little, tiny little house in the woods the animals showed Snow White. But no one was home, and when she looked in the window, my, what an untidy sight met her eyes! The sink was piled with unwashed dishes, and everything was thickly blanketed with dust.

"Maybe the children who live here need someone to keep house for them," said Snow White. "Let's clean their house."

So in they went. And with the help of her new forest friends, Snow White soon had the little house spic and span.

Then she went upstairs and fell asleep across the seven little beds.

As she slept, home from work came the seven little men who lived in that house in the woods.

"Hi-ho, hi-ho,
It's home from work we go!"

sang the seven little men—the Seven Dwarfs.

Then they saw their little house, just as Snow White had seen it. But they knew at once that something was changed! It was clean!

Up the stairs crept the Seven Dwarfs. And there they found Snow White just waking up.

"Oh!" cried Snow White. "I know who you are." She had read their names on their beds. "You're Dopey and Sneezy and Happy and Grumpy and Doc and Bashful and Sleepy!"

How pleased they all were to think that she knew their names! All except Grumpy.

"Ask her who she is," Grumpy said, "and what she's doing here."

"Oh, I forgot to tell you. I'm Snow White."

"The Princess!" whispered the Seven Dwarfs.

So she told them all about the wicked Queen's plot, and the dwarfs insisted that she stay.

"Supper is not quite ready yet," said Snow White, who was ever so pleased to be asked to stay. "You'll just have time to wash."

"Wash?" cried all the little men. It had been so long since any of them had washed that they had almost forgotten what the word meant.

"Let me see your hands," said Snow White. What hands! Even the dwarfs were embarrassed. Sheepishly they filed out and began to suds their faces and their hands. All but Grumpy.

"Humph," said Grumpy. "I'd like to see anybody make me wash."

He scrambled up onto a barrel and sulked.

"All right," said Doc. "Grab him, men."

Into the tub they tossed Grumpy, kicking and yelling, and three men held him down while the other three scrubbed.

"Supper!" called Snow White from the doorway.

They all dropped Grumpy and ran. For fresh-baked biscuits and gooseberry pie didn't come their way every day.

MEANWHILE, BACK AT the castle, the huntsman had presented to the wicked Queen the box, which she thought contained Snow White's heart.

"Ahhh!" she gloated. "At last!"

Then down the castle corridors she hurried straight to the magic mirror.

"Now, magic mirror on the wall,
Who is the fairest one of all?"

The mirror replied:

"With the Seven Dwarfs will spend the night
The fairest in the land, Snow White!"

Then the Queen realized that the huntsman had tricked her. In anger, she hurled the box at the mirror, shattering it into a thousand pieces. Still shaking with rage, the Queen hurried through damp tunnels to a dark cave far below the palace. There she pushed open the heavy door to her laboratory, where she worked her Black Magic.

She opened a book entitled *Magic Disguises.* Keeping one trembling finger on the chosen page, she stirred up a weird potion, and when it was ready she drank it down.

The beautiful Queen disappeared, and in her place stood a toothless old hag in tattered rags. She made her way to the river beneath the castle and stepped into a boat.

"And now for the Princess," cackled the ugly creature. "What shall it be? The poisoned apple, the Sleeping Death—perfect!"

Back in the forest, Snow White and the dwarfs had forgotten all about the cruel Queen.

They spent a happy evening—the happiest of the little men's lives—playing and singing and dancing about.

When the fire burned low and the clock struck eleven, Snow White hurried the little men off to sleep. They insisted that she have their beds again.

In the morning they felt a little stiff from sleeping on the floor. But Snow White made them

all feel better by kissing them good-bye as they marched away to work.

"Be careful of strangers," said Grumpy with a scowl. And Snow White promised she would.

She went back to her housekeeping, happy as could be.

The seven little men did not go to work that day. They spent their time building a bed for Snow White. But they would not have worked so merrily, if they could have seen the wicked Queen making her way to their very own house with a poisoned apple for Snow White!

Snow White quite forgot her promise to beware of strangers when the little old woman stopped at her door.

"Here's a Magic Wishing Apple, my dear," the old woman said. "One bite, and your wish will come true."

"Oh," said Snow White, thinking of the handsome Prince of her dreams, "thank you."

She bit into the apple and immediately sank to the floor, lifeless.

"Now I am the fairest in the land!" croaked the wicked Queen. "Nothing but Love's First Kiss can save her, and her love will never find her now."

Away hurried the wicked Queen, just as the dwarfs came home. They recognized her through all her disguise, and they chased her through the woods until she slipped on a ledge and fell into a chasm far below.

But that did not bring Snow White back to life. The sad dwarfs built her a new bed all made of crystal and gold. They laid it on a grassy knoll in the forest. There they kept watch over her night and day.

Now a handsome Prince of a nearby kingdom heard of the lovely Princess sleeping in the forest, and he rode there to see her.

Instantly her beauty charmed the Prince's heart, and he loved her dearly. So he knelt beside the bed and kissed her lips.

At the touch of Love's First Kiss, Snow White awoke. There, bending over her, was the Prince of her dreams. Snow White knew that she loved him. She said good-bye to the Seven Dwarfs and, mounted on a white charger behind her Prince, rode off to his Castle of Dreams Come True.

Cinderella

ADAPTED BY CAMPBELL GRANT
FROM THE WALT DISNEY MOTION PICTURE "CINDERELLA"

ONCE UPON A TIME in a faraway land lived a sweet and pretty girl named Cinderella. She made her home with her mean old stepmother and her two stepsisters, and they made her do all the work in the house.

Cinderella cooked and baked. She cleaned and scrubbed. She had no time left for parties and fun.

But one day an invitation came from the palace of the king. A great ball was to be given for the prince of the land. And every young girl in the kingdom was invited.

"How nice!" thought Cinderella. "I am invited, too."

But her mean stepsisters never thought of her.

They thought only of themselves, of course. They had all sorts of jobs for Cinderella to do.

"Wash this slip. Press this dress. Curl my hair. Find my fan."

They both kept shouting, as fast as they could speak.

"But I must get ready myself. I'm going, too," said Cinderella.

"You!" they hooted. "You want to go to the Prince's ball?"

And they kept her busy all day long. She worked in the morning, while her stepsisters slept. She worked all afternoon, while they bathed and dressed. And in the evening she had to help them put on the finishing touches for the ball. She had not one minute to think of herself.

Soon the coach was ready at the door. The ugly stepsisters were powdered, pressed, and curled. But there stood Cinderella in her workaday rags.

"Why, Cinderella!" said the stepsisters. "You're not dressed for the ball."

"No," said Cinderella. "I guess I cannot go."

Poor Cinderella sat weeping in the garden.

Suddenly a little old woman with a sweet,

kind face stood before her. It was her fairy god-mother.

"Hurry, child!" she said. "You are going to the ball!"

Cinderella could hardly believe her eyes! The fairy godmother turned a fat pumpkin into a splendid coach with magic words and with the touch of her wand.

Next Cinderella's pet mice became horses,

and her dog a fine footman. The barn horse was turned into a coachman.

"There, my dear," said the fairy godmother. "Now into the coach with you, and off to the ball you go."

"But my dress—" said Cinderella.

"Lovely, my dear," the fairy godmother be-gan. Then she really looked at Cinderella's rags.

"Oh, good heavens," she said. "You can never go in that." She waved her magic wand, and said:

> "Salaga doola,
> Menchicka boola,
> Bibbidy bobbidy boo!"

There stood Cinderella in the loveliest ball dress that ever was. And on her feet were tiny glass slippers!

"Oh," cried Cinderella. "How can I ever thank you?"

"Just have a wonderful time at the ball, my dear," said her fairy godmother. "But remember, this magic lasts only until midnight. At the stroke of midnight, the spell will be broken. And every-thing will be as it was before."

"I will remember," said Cinderella.

Then into the magic coach she stepped and was whirled away to the ball.

And such a ball! The king's palace was ablaze with lights. There was music and laughter. And every lady in the land was dressed in her beautiful best.

But Cinderella was the loveliest of them all. The prince never left her side all evening long. They danced every dance. They had supper side by side. And they smiled happily into each other's eyes.

But all at once the clock began to strike midnight, Bong Bong Bong—

"Oh!" cried Cinderella. "I almost forgot!"

And without a word, away she ran, out of the ballroom and down the palace stairs. She lost one of her glass slippers. But she could not stop.

Into her magic coach she stepped, and away it rolled. But as the clock stopped striking, the coach disappeared. And no one knew where she had gone.

Next morning all the kingdom was filled with the news. The Grand Duke was going from house to house with a small glass slipper in his hand. For the prince had said he would marry no one but the girl who could wear that tiny shoe.

Every girl in the land tried hard to put it on. The ugly stepsisters tried hardest of all. But not a one could wear the glass shoe.

"Please!" cried Cinderella. "Please let me try."

And of course the slipper fitted, since it was her very own.

That was all the Duke needed. Now his long search was over. And so Cinderella became the prince's bride, and lived happily ever after—and the little pet mice lived in the palace and were happy ever after, too.

And where was Cinderella? Locked in her room. For the mean old stepmother was taking no chances of letting her try on the slipper. Poor Cinderella! It looked as if the Grand Duke would surely pass her by.

But her little friends, the mice, got the stepmother's key. And they pushed it under Cinderella's door. So down the long stairs she came, as the Duke was just about to leave.

Alice in Wonderland

MEETS THE WHITE RABBIT

RETOLD BY JANE WERNER

ADAPTED BY AL DEMPSTER FROM THE MOTION PICTURE
BASED ON THE STORY BY LEWIS CARROLL

Do YOU KNOW where Wonderland is? It is the place you visit in your dreams, the strange and wondrous place where nothing is as it seems. It was in Wonderland that Alice met the White Rabbit.

He was hurrying across the meadow, looking at his pocket watch and saying to himself, "I'm late, I'm late, for an important date."

So Alice followed him.

"What a peculiar place to give a party," she thought as she pushed her way into the hollow tree.

But before she could think any more, she began to slide on some slippery white pebbles inside.

And then

"Curious and curiouser!" said Alice as she floated slowly down, past cupboards and lamps, a rocking chair, past clocks and mirrors she met in mid-air.

By the time she reached the bottom, and landed with a thump, the White Rabbit was disappearing through a tiny little door, too small for Alice to follow him.

Poor Alice! She was all alone in Wonderland, where nothing was just what it seemed. (You know how things are in dreams!)

she   began   to   *fall!*

At last she reached a neat little house in the woods, with pink shutters and a little front door that opened and—out came the White Rabbit!

She met other animals, yes, indeed, strange talking animals, too. They tried to be as helpful as they could. But they couldn't help her find the White Rabbit.

"And I really must find him," Alice thought, though she wasn't sure just why.

So on she wandered through Wonderland, all by her lonely self.

"Oh, my twitching whiskers!" he was saying to himself. He seemed very much upset. Then he looked up and saw Alice standing there.

"Mary Ann!" he said sharply. "Why, Mary Ann, what are you doing here? Well, don't just do something, stand there! No, go get my gloves. I'm very late!"

"But late for what? That's just what I—"
Alice began to ask.

"My gloves!" said the White Rabbit firmly.
And Alice dutifully went to look for them, though
she knew she wasn't Mary Ann!

When she came back, the White Rabbit was
just disappearing through the woods again.

So off went Alice, trying to follow him through
that strange, mixed-up Wonderland.

She met Tweedledee and Tweedledum, a funny
little pair.

She joined a mad tea party with the Mad
Hatter and the March Hare.

She met a Cheshire cat who faded in and out
of sight. And one strange creature—Jabberwock—
whose eyes flamed in the night.

They all were very kind, but they could not
show Alice the way, until—

"There *is* a short cut," she heard the Cheshire
cat say. So Alice took it.

The short cut led into a garden where gardeners
were busy painting roses red.

"We must hurry," they said, "for the Queen
is coming!"

And sure enough, a trumpet blew, and a voice called:

"Make way for the Queen of Hearts!"

Then out came a grand procession. And who should be the royal trumpeter for the cross-looking Queen but the White Rabbit, all dressed up and looking very fine.

"Well!" said Alice. "So this is why he was hurrying so!"

"Who are you?" snapped the Queen. "Do you play croquet?"

"I'm Alice. And I'm just on my way home. Thank you for the invitation, but I really mustn't stay."

"So!" cried the Queen. "So she won't play! Off with her head then!"

But Alice was tired of Wonderland now, and all its nonsensical ways.

"Pooh!" she said. "I'm not frightened of you. You're nothing but a pack of cards."

And with that she ran back through that land of dreams, back to the river bank where she had fallen asleep.

"Hm," she said, as she rubbed her eyes. "I'm glad to be back where things are what they seem. I've had quite enough for now of Wonderland!"

Peter Pan
and Wendy

TOLD BY ANNIE NORTH BEDFORD

ADAPTED BY EYVIND EARLE

Once upon a time there were three children, Wendy, John, and Michael Darling by name.

They liked bedtime, because every night in the nursery Wendy told stories about Peter Pan. Peter is a little boy who decided never to grow up.

He lives in a faraway Never Land, full of adventure and fun.

The children loved to hear stories about him.

And Peter Pan himself (with the fairy, Tinker Bell) would come flying down and sit on the nursery windowsill to hear the stories. One night Peter asked the children to come with him to the Never Land.

Wendy was delighted. And Peter taught them how to fly—it was as easy as one, two, three. All it took was a wish and pinch of pixie dust—and a little practice, too.

Then out the nursery window they flew, and away to the Never Land.

The Never Land was a wonderful place—an island in a nameless sea.

There were fairies living in the treetops.

There were mermaids swimming in a lagoon. There were real Indians in a village on a cliff. There were woods full of wild animals.

Best of all, there was a shipful of pirates— wicked ones, with an especially wicked leader, Captain Hook.

Wendy, John, and Michael knew at first sight that they would love the Never Land. And they did.

They liked Peter's wonderful underground house, with lots of hidden doorways in a great big hollow tree. There they met the Lost Boys who shared Peter's home. And the Boys were delighted that Wendy had come to tell bedtime stories to them.

But they did not spend much time in that underground house. There were too many exciting things to do.

Sometimes they played at war with the Indians, who were really their very good friends.

Sometimes they had trouble with the wicked pirates, who were their enemies.

One day the pirates stole away Princess Tiger Lily of the Indian tribe.

The Indian Chief, her father, was all upset. But Peter Pan rescued Tiger Lily and brought her safely home again.

That made Captain Hook, the leader of the pirates, madder at Peter Pan than he had ever been.

"I'll catch that Pan if it's the last thing I do!" he vowed. And he laid a wicked plan.

He kidnapped Wendy, John, and Michael and all the Lost Boys while Peter was away. And he took them to his pirate ship.

"Now, my fine fellows," said Captain Hook, when he had the Boys and Wendy on his ship, "which will it be? Will you all turn pirates, or do you want to walk the plank, and fall *kerplash* into the sea?"

"I guess we'll turn pirates," said the Boys.

But Wendy would have none of that.

"I think you should be ashamed of yourselves," she said. "Peter Pan will rescue us."

And she was right. For at the last minute Peter Pan appeared.

He beat Captain Hook in a good, fair fight, and he freed every one of his friends. They scared those bad pirates into jumping overboard and rowing away in their boat.

"Hurrah!" cried Pan. "Now the pirate ship is ours!"

"Where shall we sail to?" cried the Boys.

"It's time we went home," Wendy said.

"If you must go home, we'll sail there," said Peter Pan.

With a wish and a pinch of pixie dust, they made the pirate ship fly! And away they all sailed on that ship, through the sky, to the nursery window again.

The children's parents could scarcely believe that their children had been to the Never Land. But Wendy, John, and Michael, even when they grew up, never forgot Peter Pan.

Cinderella's FRIENDS

TOLD BY JANE WERNER

FROM THE MOTION PICTURE "CINDERELLA"

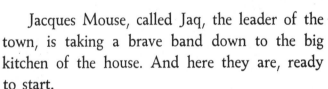

TWEET! TWEET! It is morning. At the bluebird's song, Mouse Town, in the garret of Cinderella's house, wakes up with a squeak and a yawn.

Today is the day of the great Mouse Ball. Everyone is busy. The mice ladies are decking out the town. Even the bluebirds have come to help and to join in the chorus of the merry mouse song. And this is what they sing:

> *"Cinderella, Cinderella,*
> *Is the sweetest one of all.*
> *Now she's marrying her prince and*
> *So we're having a great ball!"*

Yes, the lady mice have the decorations well in hand. And the men are to provide the food.

Jacques Mouse, called Jaq, the leader of the town, is taking a brave band down to the big kitchen of the house. And here they are, ready to start.

"Be careful!" call the lady mice, waving pocket handkerchiefs. "Be sure to watch out for the cat!"

"We will!" the men promise. For they know that cat—the fat and evil Lucifer. But they are brave mice. Away they march, right through a hole in the wall.

Down, down, down dark tunnels they make their way. And as they march they sing a song:

> *"Cinderella, Cinderella,*
> *Is the princess of the land,*
> *And to make her ball a fine one,*
> *We will lend a helping hand."*

At last they stop. They have come to the kitchen of the house. "Sh!" says Jaq. And the song breaks off as Jaq creeps out for a look around.

There in the coziest spot of all, close to the fire, lies Lucifer Cat. But he is fast asleep.

"Come on!" Jaq signals. And out they creep.

Here come the mice, all set for a climb. One, two, three, up to the chair. Four, five, six, to the table top. And they load themselves down with as much food as they can hold.

Then six, five, four, to the kitchen floor, and back, back, back toward the hole they go. But plump and greedy Gus spies one more piece of cheese. He can't pass it up. He reaches, and *snap!* Gus finds himself tight in a mouse trap.

Snap! Lucifer awakes! He opens one eye. The mice have vanished, all but Gus.

"Aha!" purrs Lucifer, with a horrid, hungry smile. He reaches out a paw, but it is not long enough.

"Ho hum," yawns Lucifer to himself. "Someone will come soon and open the trap. I can have my feast then. I'll finish my nap."

"Zzzzzz," snores Lucifer Cat. And out from their hiding places all around, hush-hush-hush, creep the mice.

They shake their heads at greedy Gus. But one, two, three, they spring that trap!

And out comes Gus with a *ping!*

Ping! Up wakes Lucifer, and there are the mice. "Aha!" he snarls. "I've got you now!" And he springs!

"Hurry, men!" cries Jaq. "Into the wall!" The mice race for the wall, carrying what they

24

can. Jaq stays behind to manage Lucifer. And he leads the cat a merry chase.

Into the hole in the wall they climb, one, two, three—mouse after mouse with loads of food.

Now it's Gus's turn, with his grapes piled high. But he has too many. *Plink, plunk, scatter,* down they fall!

Poor Jaq. He is wearing out. Lucifer is coming close. Gus sees his friend's danger. But what can he do?

Squish! He steps on a grape. It hits Lucifer in the eye. While he screeches with rage, *zip!* up go Jaq and Gus.

Then up, up, up through the walls they go, a happy band of mice. As they climb, they sing a happy song. And this is the song they sing:

"Cinderella,
 Cinderella,
How we'll celebrate
 tonight!
We will feast and
 dance and frolic
By the moon and
 candlelight!"

And they did! You have never seen such a beautiful place as Mouse Town was that night. There has never been a more wonderful feast, with dancing and singing and cheering.

And that's how Cinderella's mice celebrated her wedding to the prince.

MICKEY MOUSE
AND PLUTO PUP

MICKEY MOUSE CAME down the stairs whistling. He planned on a fine day's fishing with his loyal Pluto Pup.

He fixed a big dog breakfast in Pluto Pup's own bowl. Then he whistled for Pluto at the back door. But Pluto did not come.

Mickey looked everywhere for Pluto. Then he noticed that the back gate was open.

"Aha!" thought Mickey. "That's the answer. Pluto has gone to see Minnie, I'll bet."

So Mickey Mouse jumped into his car and drove to Minnie's house.

"I came for Pluto," Mickey said, when Minnie came to the door. "Is he here?"

"Why, no," said Minnie. "Do you suppose he's lost? I'll come and help you look for him."

So Mickey and Minnie jumped into the car and drove to Donald Duck's house, where Donald was out raking leaves.

"We've come for Pluto," they told Donald Duck. "Is he here with you?"

"Why, no," said Donald. "Is he lost? I'll help you look for him."

So Donald Duck jumped into the car.

"Hey, Uncle Donald!"

"Hey, Uncle Mickey!"

"Where are you going?"

There came Donald's nephews, one, two, three—Huey, Louie, and Dewey, on the run.

"We're going to look for Pluto," Donald said.

"Can we come along?"

"Okay," said Mickey. So in they piled. And they all rode over to Clarabelle Cow's.

Clarabelle Cow was out picking tomatoes. She straightened up and waved when she saw them.

"Hello," she called. "How are you all?"

"Fine," called the nephews. "But we can't find Pluto Pup."

"Oh, dear," said Clarabelle. "I'll help you look for him."

So into the car she climbed.

Soon they met Goofy on the street.

"Gawsh," said Goofy. "Where are you folks all headed for today?"

"Come along," said Mickey. And Goofy got into the car.

"Pluto might have gone to Horace Horse-collar's house," said Minnie.

"We'll soon see," Mickey said.

Horace had not seen Pluto Pup, but he was glad to come along to look.

All around the town they drove. Mickey drove very slowly, and they whistled and they called. But Pluto never answered them.

"Wait!" cried the nephews, all at once. "Stop here a minute, Uncle Mickey, please."

Mickey stopped. They all listened. Sure enough, from a big tent came all sorts of woofs and barks.

"The Dog Show!" cried Mickey. "Why didn't we think of that?"

"Looking for Pluto," Mickey called. "Have you seen Pluto Pup?"

"Nope," said Goofy. "But I'll help you look for him."

He parked the car and they all hurried in.

The Dog Show was almost over. Blue ribbons had been given to the best of the spaniels, the best of the terriers, to the best of the poodles, and work dogs and hounds. Now there was just one

blue ribbon left. It was for the Most Popular Dog in the Show.

As the dogs started marching past the judges' platform, who should come marching along with the rest but Mickey Mouse's Pluto Pup! He was holding his head very high.

"Pluto!" cried Mickey.

"There he is!" cried Mickey's friends.

And Pluto Pup was wild with joy. He jumped and cavorted. He rolled his eyes and flapped his ears. Everyone at the Dog Show began to laugh and clap.

The judges were impressed.

Soon Pluto had a blue ribbon all his own for being the Most Popular Dog in the Show.

Then everyone piled back into Mickey's car— with Pluto in the midst of them. And they all went back to Mickey's house, to celebrate the triumph with lots of ice cream and cake.

DONALD DUCK'S
Toy Sailboat

TOLD BY ANNIE NORTH BEDFORD

ADAPTED BY SAMUEL ARMSTRONG
FROM THE MOTION PICTURE "CHIPS AHOY"

"THERE!" said Donald Duck. "At last it's done!"

He stood back to look at his toy sailboat. Making it had been a big job. It had taken him all summer long. But now the boat was finished. And it was a beautiful boat.

The mantel was just the place for it, too. The whole room looked better with the sailboat up there.

"Building sailboats is hungry work," Donald said to himself. So he fixed himself a fine big lunch.

"Now to try out the boat in the lake," he thought. But his hard work had made him sleepy,

too. So Donald settled down for a nap after lunch.

Now outside Donald's cottage in the old elm tree, lived two little chipmunks, Chip and Dale. And they had had no lunch at all.

"I'm hungry," said Chip, rubbing his empty middle.

"Me too," said little Dale. But suddenly he brightened. "Look!" he said.

Chip looked and looked. At last he spied it— one lone acorn still clinging to the bough of an oak down beside the lake.

Down the elm tree they raced, across to the oak, and up its rough-barked trunk.

"Mine!" cried Chip, reaching for the nut.

"I saw it first!" Dale cried.

So they pushed and they tugged and they tussled, until the acorn slipped through their fingers and fell *kerplunk* into the lake.

The two little chipmunks looked mighty sad as they watched the acorn float away. But Dale soon brightened. "Look!" he cried.

Chip looked. On a little island out in the

"I don't know," said Dale. But he soon had an idea. "Look in there!" he said.

On the mantel in Donald Duck's cottage, they could see the toy sailboat.

"Come on," said Dale. So away they raced.

They had the sailboat down and almost out the door when Donald stirred in his sleep.

"Nice day for a sail," he said dreamily, as the boat slipped smoothly past his eyes.

Soon after, Donald woke up completely.

"Now to try out my boat!" he cried.

Suddenly something outside the window caught his eye. It was his sailboat, out on the lake!

"I'll fix those chipmunks!" Donald said.

He pulled out his fishing rod and reel and chose a painted fly. It looked just like a nut.

"This will do," Donald grinned.

From the pier he cast—as far as he could fling that little fishing fly. With a *plop* it landed beside the toy boat.

"Look! Look at this!" cried Dale. He leaned way over the edge of the boat to pull in the floating fly.

middle of the lake stood a great big oak tree weighted down with acorns on every side.

Down to the shore the chipmunks ran. But br-r-r! It was too cold to swim.

"How can we get to them?" wondered Chip.

"Good! A nut!" said Chip. "We'll toss it in the hold and have it for supper tonight."

As soon as it was fast in the hold, Donald pulled in the line. He pulled that little boat right in shore. The chipmunks never suspectd a thing. They did not even notice Donald pouring water into the cabin of the boat.

Chip discovered that when he went into the cabin. "Man the pumps!" he cried.

Those two chipmunks worked with might and main while Donald watched and laughed.

"Ha ha!" At Donald's chuckle, the chipmunks looked up.

"So that's the trouble!" Dale cried.

He pulled out the fishing fly from the hold and flung it at Donald so that he was soon tangled up in fishing line.

While Donald tried to tug himself free, the chipmunks set sail once more.

Before Donald could launch his swift canoe, they had touched at the island's shore.

As Donald was paddling briskly along, he heard a brisk *rat-a-tat-tat!*

The oak tree on the island seemed to shiver and shake as its store of acorns rained down. The busy little chipmunks finished dancing on the branches. Then they hauled their harvest on board.

"Oh, well," said Donald, watching from his canoe. "At least I know the sailboat really will sail. Now let's just see what those little fellows do."

And can you guess what the chipmunks did? They stored their nuts in a hollow tree. And they took Donald's toy sailboat right back, and put it where it belonged!

Winnie-the-Pooh

MEETS GOPHER

Based on a story by A. A. Milne

Adapted by

GEORGE DESANTIS

WINNIE-THE-POOH lived in the forest under the name Sanders, which means he had the name Sanders over the door and he lived *under* it.

One day when Pooh was sitting resting, his clock chimed.

"Now what does that mean?" wondered Pooh.

He knew it meant something, but being a bear of little brain, he had to think and think.

Ah yes, that was it. It was time for his stoutness exercises. Up-down, up-down went Pooh, humming a little hum.

Doing his stoutness exercises always made Pooh hungry

Oh bother. The honey pot was empty again. There was nothing in it. He would have to go out and find some.

And so Pooh went out walking and he came to a sandy bank with a hole in it. It was Rabbit's hole. And Rabbit might say, "What about a bit of lunch?"

"Is anybody at home?" called Pooh.

"NO!" said a voice.

"Bother," said Pooh. "Isn't that you, Rabbit?"

"NO!" said the voice.

Pooh stuck his head in the hole.

"Oh hello, Pooh," said Rabbit. "What a pleasant surprise. What about a bit of lunch?"

"I *do* feel like a little something, now that I come to think of it," said Pooh. And he settled down to a large small helping of honey and condensed milk (without the bread).

For a long time Pooh ate and ate and ate.

Then, in rather a sticky voice, he said goodbye to Rabbit and started to climb out of the hole.

"Oh help. Oh bother. I'm stuck," said Pooh.

"It all comes of eating too much," said Rabbit, and he started pushing. But it was no help.

"It all comes from not having front doors big enough," said Pooh.

"I shall go and fetch Christopher Robin," said Rabbit, dashing out of the back door. "Don't go away."

"I say, are you stuck?" said Owl, who had landed nearby.

"No, I'm just resting and thinking," said Pooh.

Owl looked at him closely. "You, sir, are stuck," he said. "This situation obviously calls for an expert."

"Here I am," said Samuel J. Gopher. "An excavation expert, at your service."

Gopher strutted around Pooh, poking and prodding.

"Hmm . . . hard digging . . . danger of a cave-in . . . need planks for bracing . . . big job . . . two or three days . . ."

"Two or three days?" said Pooh. "What about lunches?"

"No problem," said Gopher. "Always bring my own lunch. Run into money . . . strictly cash . . . think it over . . . let me know . . . here's my card."

And he disappeared as suddenly as he had come.

"Cheer up, Pooh Bear, we're coming," called a voice. Christopher Robin and Kanga and Roo and Piglet and Eeyore and Rabbit appeared over the hill. They started pulling and pulling.

"There's only one thing to do," said Christopher Robin, at last. "We'll have to wait until you get thin."

"Might take weeks. Or even months," said Eeyore sadly.

"And no meals," said Christopher Robin.

And so there was Winnie-the-Pooh, half in and half out of Rabbit's hole.

Night fell and rain fell, and when Pooh got wet Rabbit and the others had to wring him out.

They sang him Sustaining Songs and tried to cheer him up, and Pooh tried not to think of eating.

Then they all went home and Pooh was left alone.

"I still think I could blast you out of there," said Gopher, appearing suddenly. "You *are* that stuck-up bear, aren't you?" he added.

"Mm," said Pooh absently, eyeing Gopher's lunch box.

"What's in that box?" said Pooh, suspecting something.

"Let me see," said Gopher busily, "there's a little cold salmon and some custard and ah—oh yes, some honey—"

"Honey?" breathed Pooh.

"Honey?" gasped Rabbit, inside his hole. "Oh no! Not that!"

Finding his front door still full he dashed out by the back door and ran around just in time to see. . . .

. . . Gopher politely handing Pooh a fat jar of honey.

"Stop it at once," said Rabbit, snatching away the jar. "Not one drop."

"But Rabbit, I wasn't going to eat it," said Pooh in an offended tone of voice. "Only taste it."

"I will taste it," Rabbit said grandly. "You are in a predicament. No tasting. No eating. Till you are thin."

Thoughtfully he tasted the honey, then gave the jar back to Gopher. "Very good. In fact, not bad at all. But not for Pooh Bear."

Rabbit was quite busy for a long time, down in his hole.

When he came up he had a sign which he had made.

The sign said,
DON'T FEED THE BEAR.

Gopher didn't come back after that.

Pooh got thinner and thinner until at last, when they all pulled, and Rabbit pushed, POP! out came Pooh, and off he went flying through the air.

Christopher Robin and Piglet and Eeyore and Kanga and Roo all landed in a heap.

"Where is he?" said Rabbit looking out from his front door at last.

"Stuck again," said Eeyore sadly.

"Don't worry, silly old bear," said Christopher Robin in a loving voice. "We'll get you out."

"There's no hurry," mumbled Pooh Bear. "This is the right kind of tree and the right kind of bee."

What a happy ending for Pooh!

The Three Little Pigs

ADAPTED BY MILT BANTA AND AL DEMPSTER

from the Walt Disney Motion Picture
"The Three Little Pigs"

And as he danced he sang:

> *"I built my house of sticks,*
> *I built my house of twigs.*
> *With a hey diddle-diddle*
> *I play on my fiddle,*
> *And dance all kinds of jigs."*

Then off danced the two little pigs down the road together to see how their brother was getting along.

The third little pig was a sober little pig. He was building a house, too, but he was building his of bricks. He did not mind hard work, and he

ONCE UPON A TIME there were three little pigs who went out into the big world to build their homes and seek their fortunes.

The first little pig did not like to work at all. He quickly built himself a house of straw.

Then off he danced down the road, to see how his brothers were getting along.

The second little pig was building himself a house, too. He did not like to work any better than his brother, so he had decided to build a quick and easy house of sticks.

Soon it was finished, too. It was not a very strong little house, but at least the work was done. Now the second little pig was free to do what he liked.

What he liked to do was to play his fiddle and dance. So while the first little pig tooted his flute, the second little pig sawed away on his fiddle, dancing as he played.

wanted a stout little, strong little house, for he knew that in the woods nearby there lived a big bad wolf who liked nothing better than to catch little pigs and eat them up!

So slap, slosh, slap! Away he worked, laying bricks and smoothing mortar between them.

"Ha ha ha!" laughed the first little pig, when he saw his brother hard at work.

Just as the first pig reached his door, out of the woods popped the big bad wolf!

The little pig squealed with fright and slammed the door.

"Little pig, little pig, let me come in!" cried the wolf.

"Ho ho ho!" laughed the second little pig. "Come down and play with us!" he called.

But the busy little pig did not pause. Slap, slosh, slap! went bricks on mortar as he called down to them:

> *"I build my house of stones.*
> *I build my house of bricks.*
> *I have no chance*
> *To sing and dance,*
> *For work and play don't mix."*

"Ho ho ho! Ha ha ha!" laughed the two lazy little pigs, dancing along to the tune of the fiddle and the flute.

"You can laugh and dance and sing," their busy brother called after them, "but I'll be safe and you'll be sorry when the wolf comes to the door!"

"Ha ha ha! Ho ho ho!" laughed the two little pigs again, and they disappeared into the woods singing a merry tune:

> *"Who's afraid of the big bad wolf,*
> *The big bad wolf, the big bad wolf?*
> *Who's afraid of the big bad wolf?*
> *Tra la la la la-a-a-a!"*

"Not by the hair of my chinny-chin-chin!" said the little pig.

"Then I'll huff and I'll puff and I'll blow your house in!" roared the wolf.

And he did. He blew the little straw house all to pieces!

Away raced the little pig to his brother's house of sticks. No sooner was he in the door, when knock, knock, knock! There was the big bad wolf!

But of course, the little pigs would not let him come in.

"I'll fool those little pigs," said the big bad wolf to himself. He left the little pig's house. And he hid behind a big tree.

Soon the door opened and the two little pigs peeked out. There was no wolf in sight.

"Ha ha ha! Ho ho ho!" laughed the two little pigs. "We fooled him."

Then they danced around the room, singing gaily:

"Who's afraid of the big bad wolf,
The big bad wolf, the big bad wolf?
Who's afraid of the big bad wolf?
Tra la la la la-a-a-a!"

Soon there came another knock at the door. It was the big bad wolf again, but he had covered himself with a sheepskin, and was curled up in a big basket, looking like a little lamb.

"Who's there?" called the second little pig.

"I'm a poor little sheep, with no place to sleep.

Please open the door and let me in," said the big bad wolf in a sweet little voice.

The little pig peeked through a crack of the door, and he could see the wolf's big black paws and sharp fangs.

Soon the other two little pigs were singing and dancing with him.

This made the big bad wolf perfectly furious!

"Now by the hair of my chinny-chin-chin!" he roared, "I'll huff, and I'll puff, and I'll blow your house in!"

"Not by the hair of my chinny-chin-chin!"

"You can't fool us with that sheepskin!" said the second little pig.

"Then I'll huff, and I'll puff, and I'll blow your house in!" cried the angry old wolf.

So he huffed

and he *puffed*

and he PUFFED

and he HUFFED,

and he blew the little twig house all to pieces!

Away raced the two little pigs, straight to the third little pig's house of bricks.

"Don't worry," said the third little pig to his two frightened little brothers. "You are safe here."

He began to sing and dance.

So the big bad wolf huffed
and he *puffed*,
and he PUFFED
and he HUFFED,

but he could not blow down that little house of bricks!

Then he huffed and puffed some more, and he shook the little door until it rattled, but the three little pigs inside only laughed and danced and sang still more merrily.

That made the wolf angrier than ever! He could not blow the house down, or shake the door loose, or pry open a window. How could he get in? At last he thought of the chimney!

Very quietly the big bad wolf climbed up onto the roof of the little brick house and stole over to the chimney.

The little pigs inside were worried because the wolf was so silent. They knew he must be up to something. Then they heard a rattling in the chimney, and they knew the big bad wolf was planning to come down that way and eat them up!

The third little pig rushed over to the fireplace and snatched the lid off the great pot of water boiling there.

Down came the wolf, into the hot water!

With a yelp of pain he sprang straight up the chimney again, and raced away from that little house as fast as he could go!

The three little pigs saw him disappear into the deep woods, and they laughed and laughed and laughed. Then the little brick house rang with the tinkle of the piano and the toot of the flute and the sound of the fiddle as the three little pigs played and danced and sang:

"Who's afraid of the big bad wolf,
The big bad wolf, the big bad wolf?
Who's afraid of the big bad wolf?
Tra la la la la-a-a!"

But the big bad wolf did not hear them. He was hiding in his hole, deep in the woods. And he never came back again.

DUMBO

IT WAS SPRING—spring had come to the circus! Everyone was singing. Everyone was happy.

Happiest of all was Mrs. Jumbo, for in her stall in the circus train was a chubby, brand-new baby elephant. Though the other animals called the baby Dumbo, his mother loved him dearly. Even though his ears *were* big.

They lighted torches and stuck them in the ground. Men and animals came bustling out of the train. They all helped to get the circus tent up—Mrs. Jumbo's new baby helped.

By morning the rain had stopped, the tent was all set up, and the circus was busy getting ready for the big parade. The band played. Everyone fell in line.

"All aboard!" shouted the ringmaster.

After a long winter's rest, it was time to set out again on the open road.

"Toot! Toot!" whistled Casey Jones, the locomotive of the circus train.

And with a jiggety jerk and a brisk puff-puff, off sped Casey Jones! The circus was on its way!

It was dark when Casey Jones whistled and puffed into the station. Rain poured down hard, but the circus began to unload. The workmen jumped down from the freight cars.

Then off pranced the procession down the main street. There were creamy-white horses, licorice-colored seals! There were lady acrobats in pink silk tights, lions pacing in their gilded wagon-cages, elephants marching with slow, even steps.

The crowds on the sidewalk cheered. Then, suddenly, their eyes opened wide. They craned their necks. "Look . . . look!" they cried. "Look at that silly animal with the draggy ears! He can't be an elephant . . . he must be a clown!" They burst out in loud laughs.

A boy grabbed one of Dumbo's ears and pulled it hard. Then he made an ugly face and stuck out his tongue.

Mrs. Jumbo couldn't stand it. She snatched the boy up with her trunk, dropped him across the rope, and spanked him, hard.

"Help!" he cried, "Help! Help!"

"What's going on here?" cried the ringmaster and snapped his whip at Mrs. Jumbo. "Tie her down!" he yelled.

Mrs. Jumbo reared on her hind legs. But soon she was behind the bars in the prison wagon with a big sign that said: "Danger! Mad Elephant! Keep Out!"

The next day, they made Dumbo into a clown. They painted his face with a foolish grin and dressed him in a baby dress. On his head they put a bonnet. They used him in the most ridiculous act in the show—a make-believe fire. He had to jump from the top of a blazing cardboard house, down into a firemen's net. The audience thought it a great joke. But Dumbo felt disgraced.

"He's a disgrace to us," the big animals agreed, and turned their backs on him.

Hidden in a pile of hay was Timothy Mouse, the smallest animal with the circus.

"They can't treat the little fellow that way," he muttered. "Not while Timothy Mouse is around."

"Hey there, little fellow!" he called to Dumbo. "Don't be afraid. I'm your friend. I want to help you."

"Say!" he went on, staring at Dumbo's ears. "Those ears are as good as wings. I'll teach you to fly!"

Quietly Dumbo and Timothy crept out of the tent to Mother Jumbo.

Dumbo told her all about the clown act, and how unhappy he was without her and about the

Sadly, Dumbo toddled behind his mother, with his trunk clasped to her tail. He tried to hurry along faster so he wouldn't hear the laughter, but he stumbled. He tripped over his ears. Down he splashed into a puddle of mud. Now the crowds laughed even louder. Mrs. Jumbo scowled at them. She picked Dumbo up and carried him in her trunk the rest of the way.

When the parade finally came back to the tent, Mrs. Jumbo put Dumbo in her wooden bathtub, and as she scrubbed she whispered comforting words.

A gang of noisy boys came pushing in first for the afternoon show. "We want to see the elephant," they yelled, "—the one with the sailboat ears! Look . . . there he is."

wonderful idea Timothy had for making him a success.

Then sadly they said good night, and Timothy and Dumbo continued on their way.

With Timothy as teacher, Dumbo practiced running and jumping and hopping. He tried slow and fast takeoffs and standing and running jumps. He stretched out his wings and flapped them, 1-2-3-4. Then he tried the whole thing together. But hard as he tried, Dumbo could not leave the ground.

At last, almost too tired to stand, the two friends gave up and started gloomily back toward the sleeping circus.

"Don't worry, Dumbo," Timothy whispered as he curled up on Dumbo's hat brim for a good night's sleep. "We'll have you flying yet!"

When the morning sun arose, Timothy was the first to awaken. He blinked and looked up. Just above him, four old black crows sat and stared at him.

"Why . . . why . . ." yawned Timothy, rubbing his eyes. "Where am I?"

"You're up in our tree," snapped the crows crossly. "That's where you are."

"Tree?" gasped Timothy. He looked around. Sure enough, there he was, sitting on a branch.

He and Dumbo were up in a tree! The ground was far, far below. "But . . . but . . . how did we get here?" he stammered.

"How!" cackled the crows. "You and that elephant just came a-flyin' up!"

"Flying!" Timothy yelled. "Dumbo, Dumbo, wake up! Dumbo, we're up in a tree! You FLEW up here!"

Slowly Dumbo opened his eyes. He glanced down. He gulped. Then he struggled to his feet. But suddenly he slipped on the smooth tree bark and fell. Down . . . down . . . down! He bounced from branch to branch, with Timothy clinging to his trunk. Plonk! They landed in a shallow pond just underneath the tree. The crows chuckled and cawed from above.

Timothy scrambled up out of the water and wrung out Dumbo's tail. "Dumbo," he panted. "You can fly! If you can fly when you're asleep, you can fly when you're awake. Your ears, Dumbo, they're your fortune!" He grabbed one of Dumbo's wet ears and patted it. "You won't be a clown anymore. You'll be famous . . . the only flying elephant in the whole wide world!"

And Timothy and Dumbo began all over again to practice flying.

But it wasn't easy. Time after time, Dumbo tried to take off. Time after time, he sprawled out flat on his face. Soon the crows began to feel sorry for the little fellow. When Timothy told them all

a magic feather. Tell him if he holds it, he can fly." The boss crow winked and flew off.

Timothy handed Dumbo the feather and scurried up his trunk to the brim of his cap. He held his breath!

The trick worked like a charm. The very instant that Dumbo wrapped the tip of his trunk around the feather, flap . . . flap . . . flap! went his ears. Up into the air he soared like a bird! Over the tallest treetops he sailed. He glided, he

the sad things that had happened to Dumbo because of his big ears, they flew down and offered to help.

One of the crows took Timothy aside. "Flying's just like swimming," he whispered. "It's just a matter of believing that you can do it." He turned and snatched a long, black feather from his tail.

"Here, take this . . . tell the baby elephant it's

dipped, he dived. Three times he circled over the heads of cheering crows. Then he headed back to the circus grounds.

Timothy shouted, "We must keep your flying a secret—a surprise for this afternoon's show."

44

No one noticed Dumbo when he and Timothy came quietly back. It was already time for Dumbo to get into his costume. Inside the walls of a cardboard house he had to wait all through the show until fire crackled up around him.

At last Timothy leaned down and handed him the feather.

Cr . . rr . . rr . . ack! Cr . . rr . . ack! crackled the fire. The clown act was on! Flames shot up around the cardboard house. Clang! Clang! roared the clown fire engine, rushing toward the blaze.

From the far end of the ring, a redheaded mother clown came running. "Save my baby!" she screamed. "He's on the top floor!"

The firemen brought a big net and held it out. "Jump, my darling baby, jump!" shrieked the mother clown.

Dumbo jumped, but as he jumped the black feather slipped from his trunk and floated away. Now his magic was gone, and Dumbo plunged down like a stone.

Timothy saw the feather go. "The feather's a fake," he shouted to Dumbo. "You can fly!"

Dumbo heard the shout and, doubtfully, spread his ears wide. Not two feet above the net he stopped his plunge and swooped up into the air!

A mighty gasp arose from the audience. They knew it couldn't be, but it was! Dumbo was flying!

While the crowd roared its delight, Dumbo did power dives, loops, spins, and barrel rolls. He swooped down to pick up peanuts and squirted a trunkful of water on the clowns.

The keepers freed Mrs. Jumbo and brought her to the tent in triumph to see her baby fly. So all of Dumbo's worries had come to an end.

By evening, Dumbo was a hero from coast to coast.

Timothy became his manager and got Dumbo a wonderful contract with a big salary and a pension for his mother.

The circus was renamed "Dumbo's Flying Circus."

And Dumbo traveled in a special streamlined car. But best of all, he forgave everyone who had been unkind to him, for his heart was as big as his ears.

BUNNY BOOK

TOLD BY JANE WERNER

ADAPTED BY DICK KELSEY AND BILL JUSTICE

DEEP IN THE woods where the brier bushes grow, lies Bunnyville, a busy little bunny rabbit town.

And in the very center of that busy little town stands a cottage—a neat twig cottage with a neat brown roof—which is known to all as the very own home of Great Grandpa Bunny Bunny.

Great Grandpa Bunny Bunny, as every bunny knows, was the ancestral founder of the town.

He liked to tell the young bunnies who always gathered around how he and Mrs. Bunny Bunny, when they were very young, had found that very brier patch and built themselves that very same little twig house.

It was a happy life they lived there, deep in the woods, bringing up their bunny family in that little house of twigs.

And of course Daddy Bunny Bunny, as he was called then, was busy at his job, decorating Easter eggs.

As the children grew up, they helped paint Easter eggs. And soon they were all grown-up, with families of their own. And they built a ring of houses all around their parents' home.

By and by they had a town there, and they called it Bunnyville.

Now Grandpa Bunny Bunny looked for other jobs to do. He taught the young folk to paint flowers in the woods. They tried out new shades of green on mosses and ferns.

They made those woods so beautiful that People said. "The soil must be especially rich."

But the bunnies knew that it was all Grandpa Bunny Bunny's doing.

Years went by. Now there were still more families in Bunnyville. And Grandpa Bunny Bunny had grown to be Great Grandpa Bunny Bunny. Now he had so much help that he looked around for other jobs to do. He taught the bunnies to paint autumn leaves.

Through the woods they scampered with their brushes and pails. And People would say to themselves. "Never has there been so much color in these woods. The nights must be especially frosty hereabouts."

But the bunnies knew that it was all their Great Grandpa's plan.

And so it went, as the seasons rolled around. There were constantly more bunnies in that busy Bunnyville.

And Great Grandpa was busy finding jobs for them to do.

He taught them in winter to paint shadows on the snow . . . and pictures in frost on wintry window panes and to polish up the diamond lights on glittering icicles.

And between times he told stories to each crop of bunny young, around the cozy fire in his neat little twig home. The bunny children loved him and his funny bunny tales. And they loved

And now, the bunnies wondered, what would he think of next? Well, Great Grandpa stayed at home a lot those days, and thought and thought and thought.

And at last he told a secret to that season's bunny boys and girls.

"Children," Great Grandpa Bunny Bunny said, "I am going to go away. And I'll tell you what my next job will be, if you'll promise not to say."

the new and different things he found for them to do.

But at last it did seem as if he'd thought of everything! He had crews of bunnies trained to paint the first tiny buds of spring.

He had teams who waited beside cocoons to touch up the wings of new butterflies.

Some specialized in beetles, some in creeping, crawling things.

They had painted up that whole wild wood till it sparkled and gleamed.

So the bunny children promised. And Great Grandpa went away. The older bunnies missed him, and often they looked sad. But the bunny children only smiled and looked extremely wise. For they knew a secret they had promised not to tell.

Then one day a windy rainstorm pelted down on Bunnyville. Everyone scampered speedily home and stayed cozy and dry indoors.

After a while the rain slowed down to single dripping drops.

Then every front door opened, and out the bunny children ran.

"Oh, it's true!" those bunnies shouted. And they did a bunny dance. "Great Grandpa's been at work again. Come see what he has done!"

And the People walking out that day looked up in pleased surprise.

"Have you ever," they cried. "simply *ever* seen a sunset so gorgeously bright?"

The little bunnies heard them and they chuckled silently. For they knew that it was all Great Grandpa Bunny Bunny's plan.

49

DONALD DUCK AND THE WITCH

BASED ON THE MOTION PICTURE "TRICKS OR TREATS"

TOLD BY ANNIE NORTH BEDFORD

PICTURES BY THE WALT DISNEY STUDIO

ADAPTED BY DICK KELSEY

IT WAS GETTING on toward Halloween. Donald Duck and his nephews were hunting for pumpkins for jack-o-lanterns.

The day was almost over, and red and gold clouds were piling up in the sky, when they found a field that was full of pumpkins perfect for them.

They were walking back to the farm house, each with a round, ripe pumpkin in his arms, when Huey stopped them all with a shout.

"Look! A witch on a broomstick!" he cried.

They all saw a dark form streak across the sky.

"Pooh!" said Donald. "Witches, pooh! There are no witches, you know that. It must have been some sort of a bird you saw."

But the boys were not convinced.

Next day they set out to look for the witch.

They had a long, hard walk through the tangled woods. There was no path to follow, and they were not even sure just what they hoped to find.

At last they heard a cackling laugh up ahead. And what could be a surer sign of a witch than a crickling, cackling laugh?

"Sh!" said Dewey, with his fingers on his lips. And he led the way through the underbrush into the clearing beyond.

There stood a crooked little house, clearly the home of a witch. From the crooked little chimney rose a thread of smoke.

Smoke and steam rolled up in clouds from a cauldron out in front. And through the smoke came that merry, scary sound, the cackling laugh of a witch.

"Welcome, boys, welcome," said the witch's

voice. "Welcome to Witch Hazel's little home." Then she came hobbling toward them, a merry little sprite, grinning with witchery glee.

The boys were speechless with surprise.

"What can I do for you today?" Witch Hazel asked of them. "Any spells you'd like me to cast? Anybody you'd like to bewitch?" And her elbow poked Louie in the ribs, while she gave him a sly wink.

"Bewitch!" echoed Louie.

"Cast spells!" said Dewey.

"Uncle Donald!" cried Huey.

They all agreed. They told Witch Hazel how Donald refused to believe in witches.

"We'll show him!" she cackled, beckoning them close.

From the pockets of her dress she tossed bits of this and that into her steaming pot.

"A real witch's brew!" gasped Dewey Duck, as swirls of smoke in mysterious shapes began to rise and blow.

"We'll show that Donald!" Witch Hazel vowed. "You meet me here on Halloween."

Home went the boys, and they said not a word about their adventure to Donald Duck.

Donald was not surprised when the boys disappeared early on Halloween.

He was not surprised when his doorbell rang soon after dark that night. There beneath the porch light stood the boys. Donald chuckled as he recognized them through their disguises. They were dressed as witches, one and all.

"Come in," said Donald with a grin, holding his door open wide. They parked their broomsticks beside the door. (Donald rubbed his eyes as he thought he saw one jump. That, he knew, could not have been.)

In came the witches, one, two, three. No, there were one, two, three, four!

Donald was surprised, but he did not say a word as they all took seats around the room.

"Treats?" he asked, passing a tray of fancy little cakes.

"Ouch!" cried Dewey, who reached for one first. A mouse trap was stuck on his thumb.

"Wow!" cried Louie, who reached for one next. It turned out to be a jack-in-the-box.

"Glub!" gulped Huey, when he bit into his. It was all made of rubber, you see.

"Thanks," said the fourth guest with a cackling laugh. She blew at her cake, and it exploded into dust, right in Donald's face.

"Serves you right, smartie," said a voice. Donald whirled around. There were only the jack-o-lanterns sitting there, grinning saucily. But as

51

Donald looked, it seemed to him that the merry faces shook with glee.

"We must be leaving now," one witch said. "Won't you come with us, and let us return your hospitality?"

"No, thanks," said Donald, clinging to the doorknob as they all swept him out onto the porch.

It was four against one. He soon found himself astride a broomstick.

"Abracadabra, boys! Here we go!" he heard a voice cackle in his ear.

All around him he saw broomsticks fly—and to his horror Donald saw the ground sink away below him too!

Over the treetops and straight toward the moon the broomstick pointed—then down to the woods.

"Welcome to Witch Hazel's little home," he heard the cackling voice say. And down tumbled Donald—down, down, down into the witch's pot!

"Ho, ho, ho!" laughed the other three. He knew his nephews' voices all too well.

Donald gasped and sputtered. And he sizzled with rage when they hauled him out, soaking wet to the skin.

The witches did not notice. They were all doubled over, shaking with laughter.

Witch Hazel disappeared into her little house, and came back with an extra dress and hat.

"Better put on something dry," she told Donald with a grin. And he stamped off into the house.

When he came out again, a table was set close beside the bubbling pot. Three jack-o-lanterns glowed on a Halloween feast—pumpkin pie and apple tart and corn on the cob and all sorts of delicious things.

"Have a real treat, Uncle Donald," the nephews said, coming out from behind their masks.

So they all sat down and ate their fill—yes, Witch Hazel, too.

After a while, even Donald could smile.

"I still don't believe in witches," he said to Witch Hazel with a courtly bow, "But if there were any, I'd want them all to be just like you."

Mickey Mouse
The KITTEN-SITTERS

"GUESS WHAT!" said Mickey Mouse to his nephews, Morty and Ferdie. "We're going to be kitten-sitters. Minnie is going to leave Figaro the kitten with us tonight while she visits her Cousin Millie."

At that moment, there was a wild clucking and flapping and crowing from next door. Pluto the pup came racing across the lawn, with a big, angry rooster close behind him.

Pluto hid under the porch while Mickey shooed the rooster back to his own yard.

"Pluto!" scolded Minnie. "Chasing chickens again! Aren't you ashamed?"

Pluto *was* a bit ashamed, but only because he had let the rooster bully him. Creeping out from

under the porch, he wagged his tail and sheepishly tried to grin.

"I think it's a good thing Figaro is going to stay with you," said Minnie to Mickey. "Figaro

is a little gentleman. He can teach Pluto how to behave."

With that, Minnie handed her kitten to Mickey. Then she got into her car and drove away.

Minnie was scarcely out of sight, when Figaro jumped out of Mickey's arms and scampered into

the house. In the kitchen, he saw a pitcher of cream that Mickey had forgotten to put away.

One short jump up to a chair seat, followed by a second jump to the tabletop, brought Figaro right to the cream. The pitcher wobbled, then tipped over. Cream spilled and ran off the table and onto the floor.

Pluto growled a warning growl as Figaro lapped up the cream.

"Take it easy, Pluto," said Mickey, wiping up the spilled cream. "Figaro is our guest."

When Figaro heard that, he wrinkled his nose at Pluto and stuck out his little pink tongue.

Then he romped through the ashes in the fireplace and left sooty footprints on the carpet.

"Figaro's a very *messy* little guest," said Mickey's nephew Morty as he got out the vacuum cleaner.

At dinner time, Pluto ate his dog food, the way a good dog should. But no matter how Mickey and the boys coaxed, Figaro wouldn't touch the special kitty food Minnie had left for him. He did, at last, nibble some imported sardines.

"He's a *fussy* little guest," said Ferdie.

At bedtime, Pluto curled up in his basket without any complaint.

Did Figaro curl up on the fine, soft cushion Minnie had brought for him? He did not!

Instead, he got into bed with Morty and nipped at his toes. Then he got into bed with Ferdie and tickled both his ears. Finally, he bounced off to the kitchen, and the house became very still.

"Uncle Mickey," called Morty, "did you remember to close the kitchen window?"

"Oh, no!" cried Mickey. He jumped out of bed and ran to the kitchen.

The kitchen window was open, and Figaro the kitten was nowhere to be seen!

Mickey and the boys went through the house. They looked under every chair and behind every door.

"Figaro!" they called.

They went out into the yard. They looked under every bush and behind every tree.

No Figaro.

"He's really run away," Mickey decided at last. Morty and Ferdie followed Mickey back to the house, where Mickey put his coat on over his pajamas. "You two stay here," he told the boys. "Pluto and I will find Figaro. Leave the porch light on for us."

Pluto didn't wag his tail, and he didn't even try to grin as he got out of his cozy basket. But off he went to help Mickey in the search.

They went to Minnie's house first, but Figaro hadn't gone home.

Then they went to the park down the street. "Have you seen a little black and white kitten?" Mickey asked the policeman at the gate.

"I certainly have!" answered the policeman. "He was by the pond, teasing the ducks!"

Mickey and Pluto hurried to the pond.

Figaro wasn't there. He had been there, though. He had left behind some small, muddy footprints and several large, excited ducks.

Mickey and Pluto followed the trail of footprints to Main Street, where they met a crew of firemen.

"I'm looking for a black and white kitten," said Mickey to the firemen.

"Is that so?" said one of the firemen. "We just rescued a black and white kitten. He had climbed a telephone pole and couldn't get down again. He ran through that alley."

In the alley, a dairy-truck driver was busily cleaning up broken eggs in his truck.

"Have you seen a kitten?" asked Mickey.

"Have I!" said the driver. "He jumped into my truck and knocked over dozens of eggs!"

Mickey groaned as he paid for the smashed eggs.

When Mickey and Pluto finally trudged home, it was dawn. They had searched the whole town. They had even been to the police station, but they had not found Figaro.

"What will Aunt Minnie say?" asked the boys.

"I hate to think what Aunt Minnie will say," answered poor Mickey.

Before long, Minnie drove up. Mickey and the boys went out to meet her.

"Where is Figaro?" asked Minnie.

No one answered.

"Something has happened to him!" Minnie was upset, and she was angry. "Can't I trust you to watch *just one* sweet little kitten for me?"

Just then there was a loud clucking and squawking from the yard next door. At least a dozen frantic hens came flapping over the fence.

Close behind the hens came the big, angry rooster. Close behind the rooster came Figaro the kitten. Figaro's fur was rumpled, and he carried a long tail feather between his teeth.

"*There's* your sweet little kitten!" said Mickey.

"Figaro!" cried Minnie, not believing her eyes.

At the sound of her voice, Figaro skidded to a sudden stop. He sat down and mewed a gentle kitten mew. He tried quickly to smooth his dusty fur with his little pink tongue.

"He ran away last night," explained Mickey. "He teased the ducks in the park and broke the eggs in the dairy truck and . . ."

"And now he's chasing chickens!" finished Minnie.

"I hoped he'd teach Pluto some manners," Minnie went on. "Instead, Pluto has been teaching him to do those naughty things. Teasing ducks! Chasing chickens! The very idea! I'll *never* leave him here again."

"It wasn't Pluto's fault!" protested Morty.

"He didn't do anything bad," added Ferdie. "He stayed up all night, trying to find Figaro."

But Minnie wouldn't listen. She picked up Figaro, got into her car, and drove quickly away.

"Don't worry, boys," said Mickey. "We'll tell her the whole story later, when she's not so upset."

"Please don't tell her too soon," begged Morty. "As long as Aunt Minnie thinks Pluto is a naughty dog, we won't have to kitten-sit with Figaro."

Mickey smiled. "Maybe we *should* wait a little while. We could all use some peace and quiet."

"I did learn one thing," yawned Mickey as he stretched out beside Pluto under a shady tree. "There's not much sitting in kitten-sitting."

Bambi

Based on the original story by Felix Salten

ADAPTED BY BOB GRANT

FROM THE WALT DISNEY MOTION PICTURE "BAMBI"

BAMBI CAME into the world in the middle of a thicket, one of those little hidden forest glades which seem to be open but are really screened in on all sides.

The magpie was the first to discover him.

"This is quite an occasion," he said. "It isn't often that a Prince is born. Congratulations!"

Bambi's mother looked up. "Thank you," she said quietly. Then she nudged her sleeping baby gently with her nose. "Wake up," she whispered. "Wake up!"

The fawn lifted his head and looked around. He looked frightened and edged closer to his mother's body. She licked him reassuringly and nudged him again. He pushed up on his thin hind legs, trying to stand. His forelegs kept crumpling, but at last they bore his weight and he stood beside his mother.

"What are you going to name the young Prince?" asked the baby rabbit.

"I'll call him Bambi," the mother answered.

"Bambi," repeated the rabbit. "That's a good name. My name's Thumper." And he hopped away with his mother and sisters.

The little fawn sank down and nestled close to his mother. She licked his spotted red coat softly.

The birds and animals slipped away through the forest, leaving the thicket in peace and quiet.

The forest was beautiful in the summer. The trees stood still under the blue sky, and out of the earth came troops of flowers, unfolding their red, white, and yellow stars.

Bambi liked to follow his mother down the forest paths, so narrow that the thick leafy bushes stroked his flanks as he passed. Sometimes a branch tripped him or a bush tangled about his legs, but always his mother walked easily and surely.

There were friends all along these forest paths. The opossums, hanging by their long tails from the branches of a tree, said, "Hello, Prince Bambi."

As Bambi and his mother reached a little clearing in the forest, they met Thumper and his family.

"Come on, Bambi," said Thumper, "let's play."

And Bambi began to run on his stiff, spindly legs. Then he saw a family of birds on a low branch. He stared at them.

"These are birds, Bambi," Thumper said.

"Birds," said Bambi slowly. It was his first word. When he saw a butterfly flutter across the path, he cried, "Bird, bird!" again.

"No, Bambi," said Thumper. "That's not a bird. It's a butterfly."

Then Bambi saw a clump of yellow flowers, and he bounded toward them.

"Butterfly!" he cried.

"No, Bambi," said Thumper. "Flower."

Suddenly he drew back. Out from the bed of flowers came a small black head with two gleaming eyes.

"Flower!" said Bambi.

"That's not a flower," Thumper giggled. "Skunk."

"Flower," said Bambi again.

"The young Prince can call me Flower if he wants to," said the skunk. "I don't mind. In fact, I like it."

Bambi had made another friend.

One morning Bambi and his mother walked down a path where the fawn had never been. A few steps more and they would be in a meadow.

"Wait here until I call you," she said. "The meadow is not always safe."

She listened in all directions and called, "Come."

Bambi bounded out. Joy seized him and he leaped into the air, three, four, five times.

"Catch me!" his mother cried, and she bounded forward.

Bambi started after her. He felt as if he were flying, without any effort.

As he stopped for breath, he saw standing beside him a small fawn.

"Hello," she said, moving nearer to him.

Bambi, shy, bounded away to where he saw his friend, Flower the skunk, playing. He pretended he did not see the new little fawn.

"Don't be afraid, Bambi," his mother said. "That is little Faline; her mother is your Aunt Ena."

Soon Bambi and Faline were racing around hillocks.

Suddenly there was a sound of hoofbeats, and figures came bursting out of the woods. They were the stags.

One of the stags was larger and stronger than all the others. This was the great Prince of the Forest who was very brave and wise.

The great stag uttered one dreadful word: "MAN!"

Instantly birds and animals rushed toward the woods. As Bambi and his mother disappeared into the trees, they heard behind them on the meadow loud, roaring noises, terrifying to Bambi's ears.

Later, as Bambi and his mother lay safely in their thicket, his mother explained. "MAN, Bambi —it was MAN in the meadow. He brings danger and death to the forest with his long stick that roars and spurts flames. Someday you will understand."

One morning Bambi woke up shivering with cold. His nose told him there was something strange in the world. When he looked out through the thicket he saw everything covered with white.

"It's snow, Bambi," his mother said. "Go ahead and walk out."

Cautiously Bambi stepped on the surface of the snow and saw his feet sink down in it. The air was calm and the sun on the white snow sparkled. Bambi was delighted.

out onto the smooth ice, too. His front legs shot forward, his rear legs slipped back, and down he crashed! He looked up to see Thumper laughing at him.

He finally lurched to his feet and skidded across the ice dizzily, landing headfirst in a snowbank on the shore.

As he walked, stepping high and carefully, a breeze shifted a branch above him ever so slightly, just enough to tip a heavy load of snow on Bambi's head. He jumped high in the air, startled and frightened, then ran on, licking the snow from his nose. It tasted good—clean and cool.

Thumper was playing on the ice-covered pond, and Bambi trotted gingerly down the slope and

As he pulled himself out of the drift, he and Thumper heard a faint sound of snoring. Peering down into a deep burrow, they saw the little skunk lying peacefully asleep on a bed of withered flowers.

"Wake up, Flower!" Bambi called.

"Is it spring yet?" Flower asked sleepily.

"No, winter's just beginning," said Bambi.

"I'm hibernating," the little skunk said. "Flowers always sleep in the winter." And he dozed off again.

So Bambi learned about winter. It was a difficult time for all the animals in the forest. Food grew scarce. Sometimes Bambi and his mother had to strip bark from trees and eat it.

At last, when it seemed they could find no more to eat, there was a change in the air. Thin sunshine filtered through the bare branches, and the air was a little warmer. That day, too, Bambi's mother dug under the soft snow and found a few blades of pale green grass.

Bambi and his mother were nibbling at the grass when they suddenly smelled MAN. As they lifted their heads, there came a deafening roar.

"Quick, Bambi," his mother said, "run for the thicket. Don't stop, no matter what happens."

Bambi darted away and heard his mother's footsteps behind him. Then came another roar from MAN's guns. Bambi dashed among the trees in terrified speed. But when he came at last to the thicket, his mother was not in sight. He sniffed the air for her smell and listened for her hoofbeats. There was nothing!

Bambi raced out into the forest, calling wildly for his mother. Silently the old stag appeared beside him.

"Your mother can't be with you anymore," the stag said. "You must learn to walk alone."

In silence, Bambi followed the great stag off through the snow-filled forest.

It was spring. Everything was turning green, and the leaves looked fresh and smiling.

Suddenly Bambi looked up and saw another deer.

"Hello, Bambi," said the other deer. "Don't you remember me? I'm Faline." Bambi stared at her. Faline was now a graceful and beautiful doe.

A strange excitement swept over Bambi. When Faline trotted up and licked his face, Bambi started to dash away. But after a few steps, he stopped. Faline dashed into the bushes and Bambi followed.

Suddenly Ronno, a buck with big antlers, stood between Bambi and Faline.

"Stop!" he cried. "Faline is going with me."

Bambi stood still as Ronno nudged Faline down the path. Suddenly he shot forward, and they charged together with a crash.

Again and again they came together, forehead to forehead. Then a prong broke from Ronno's antlers, a terrific blow tore open his shoulder, and he fell to the ground, sliding down a rocky embankment.

As Ronno limped off into the forest, Bambi and Faline walked away through the woods. At night they trotted onto the meadow, where they stood in the moonlight, listening to the east wind and the west wind calling to each other.

Early one morning in the autumn Bambi sniffed the scent of MAN.

The great stag came and said, "Yes, Bambi, it's MAN, with tents and campfires. We must go to the hills."

Bambi ran back to the thicket for Faline. The sounds of MAN and the barking of dogs came closer.

He lunged at the dogs and called, "Run, Faline!"

The roar of a gun crashed almost beside him, but he dashed ahead as a killing pain shot through him.

The old stag appeared and said, "The forest has caught fire from the flames of MAN's campfires. We must go to the river." They plunged into the raging fire, and then fell into cool, rushing water.

Panting and breathless, they struggled onto a safe shore, already crowded with other animals.

With a cry of joy Faline came running to him and gently licked the wound on his shoulder.

Together they stood on the shore, and watched the flames destroy their forest home.

Spring had come again, and green leaves and grass and flowers covered the scars left by the fire.

Again news went through the forest. "Come along, come to the thicket."

At the thicket, the squirrels and rabbits and birds were peering through the undergrowth at Faline, and two spotted fawns.

And high above them on a cliff, Bambi stood watching—Bambi, the proud father and the new great Prince of the Forest.

THUMPER

Based on the character created by
Walt Disney for the motion picture, "BAMBI"

IN a forest high in the hills lived many animals. There were opossums and foxes, squirrels and mice. Bambi, the young deer, lived there, and so did Flower, the skunk. There were many birds too, and the wisest of them all was the owl.

But the largest family in the woods was the rabbit family. The mother rabbit had five children, and they kept her busy indeed.

There was Blossom, who had tall, beautiful ears.

There was Frilly, who was very playful. She would rather play than eat or sleep.

There was Violet, who had a bushy tail and was very shy.

There was Milly, who was always so hungry that she could never get enough to eat.

And there was Thumper.

Training a big family of rabbits is not easy, but the mother rabbit found most of her children to be very good. Of course, she wished that Milly would not eat *quite* so much, and she hoped that Violet would stop being so terribly shy. But they were all good about learning manners and obeying.

All except Thumper.

Sweet as he looked, he was a problem!

Every morning the rabbit family went to the meadow and played in the tall grass. Then they went over to a big patch of clover to eat their breakfast.

One day the mother rabbit was watching her children eat breakfast.

"Blossom, come back here and finish your meal," she called. Instead of eating, Blossom was looking into the pond and admiring the reflection of her beautiful, big ears.

Frilly was playing, as usual. "Frilly, you mustn't play with that butterfly until you've eaten two more clumps of greenery," she cried.

Then the mother rabbit noticed Thumper. Nibbling at some sweet flowers, Thumper was not even touching the green leaves.

"Thumper! The flowers are for dessert. What did the wise old owl tell you about eating the leaves first?"

Thumper hung his head, looked at the ground, and thumped his left rear foot. Then he recited what the owl had told him:

Eating greens is a special treat.
They make long ears and great big feet.

"But it sure is awful stuff to eat," he added to himself in a whisper.

Thumper's mother wanted him to eat properly, but *that* was not what worried her most. In the beautiful meadow, she could always make sure that all of her children ate enough greens.

What worried her most about Thumper was . . . his THUMPING!

Now, all of her children thumped once in a while, beating their strong rear feet against the ground. Rabbits are supposed to thump sometimes, especially when there is danger.

But Thumper thumped about everything.

He thumped when he was ashamed!

He thumped when he was hungry!

He thumped when he was angry!

And he thumped when he was happy!

Thumper really liked to thump.

But Thumper's sisters and Thumper's mother did *not* like his thumping.

"I just can't seem to help it," explained Thumper. "When something happens, I just have to thump."

One day, when the rabbit family was getting ready to go to the meadow, Thumper thumped loudly in his excitement.

"Now, this just *has* to stop!" cried his mother.

"I'll have to punish you. Today you cannot go to the meadow with us. Just stay here alone, and maybe you'll learn to control that thumping."

Thumper watched his mother and his sisters

hop away. He thumped a few thumps because he was lonely, but then he thought of his friend the owl.

At the base of the tall oak where the big bird had his nest, Thumper thumped as loudly as he could and called, "Hello, Friend Owl."

But Thumper had forgotten that it was daylight and the owl would be sound asleep.

"Stop that infernal noise!" growled the owl, yawning. "What do you mean by waking me out of a sound sleep? If you don't stop that thumping, young man, you're going to get into trouble. Now go away!"

Thumper was very sad. Even the old owl, who had always been his best friend, was angry with him.

The only thing to do, he decided, was to run away from home. Maybe somewhere else he would find friends who didn't mind his thumping.

So Thumper set off, hopping in the opposite direction from the meadow. He had never been very far that way, because his mother had told him it was dangerous. MAN, who hunted in the forest with his big hunting dogs, lived there.

Thumper didn't know anything about MAN or the dogs, except that all the animals said they were dangerous. But maybe they wouldn't care if he thumped!

After a few minutes, Thumper suddenly heard a strange sound ahead of him. He stopped and listened. Something was crashing through the forest toward him!

Thumper was frightened, so, of course, he thumped on the ground. The hunting dogs heard the thump and came running toward Thumper. And behind the dogs came the hunters!

Racing homeward, Thumper saw a hollow log and ran into it. He thumped and thumped and thumped, and the log boomed loudly.

Nearby, the frog was startled and leaped into the air. Then, when he heard the dogs barking around Thumper's hollow log, the frog was so frightened that he jumped into a nest of pheasants.

"The hunters are coming! Thumper the rabbit warned me!" cried the frog.

The pheasants flew to the oak and woke up the owl. The owl shouted to the crows, and all the birds called to the animals of the forest, "MAN! The hunters are coming! Run to the hills for safety! Thumper the rabbit has given the warning!"

But the frog and the owl told her how Thumper had warned them of the hunters.

"If it hadn't been for Thumper and his thumping," said the owl, "we would have been in terrible danger."

Then, instead of scolding Thumper, the mother rabbit beamed with pleasure. And as she took her little son home, she vowed that she would never

So the animals and the birds of the forest fled to the hills. The hunters and their dogs tramped through the forest for a long time, but all of the forest birds and animals had gotten away safely.

Finally, after several hours, the hunters went home, and the forest was quiet once more.

All the animals returned.

All but Thumper.

Thumper, very frightened by the hunters, still sat inside his hollow log.

The owl and the frog brought Thumper's mother to the log, and then Thumper came out.

The hunters were gone, but now Thumper was afraid his mother would punish him for running away from home. And, in fact, the mother rabbit *was* all ready to scold her son for giving her such a fright.

again scold him for thumping too much. All of the birds and animals of the forest agreed with her.

And now Thumper thumps whenever and wherever he likes!

SCAMP

TOLD BY ANNIE NORTH BEDFORD

ADAPTED BY NORM McGARY and JOE RINALDI

*L*ADY WAS the mother.
Tramp was the father.
Their puppies were the finest ever.
They were sure of that.
Three were as gentle and as pretty as their mother.
But the fourth little puppy—
"Where is that puppy? Where is that Scamp?" they cried.
At mealtime three little gentle pretty puppies would line up, waiting for their bowl.

But the fourth little puppy, that Scamp of a puppy, would rush in ahead of them all.
At playtime three little gentle pretty puppies would play with their own puppy toys.
But the fourth little puppy, that Scamp of a puppy, would nibble at anything.

At bedtime three gentle pretty puppies would snuggle down to sleep.
But the fourth little puppy, that Scamp of a puppy, chose that time to learn to howl, loud and long.

67

One day the four little puppies started off for a picnic with nice puppy biscuits for lunch.

Three little puppies went straight to the park and hunted for a shady spot.

But the fourth little puppy, that Scamp of a puppy, went off on an adventure.

He found some new playmates.
Their game looked like fun.
But Sss-ss-sst! they didn't want Scamp to play.
So Scamp got out of there.
He found another playmate.
It was a busy gopher, digging as fast as it could dig.

"Looks like fun," said Scamp. "How did you learn to do it?"

"By digging," Mr. Gopher said. So Scamp dug, too.

He dug and dug and dug.

And what do you think he found?

A big, juicy bone.

It was a great big bone for a small dog.

Scamp pulled at it.

He tugged and hauled.

He tugged that bone all the way down the street to the park.

Just as Scamp got there, a big bad dog was saying, "Ha! I smell puppy biscuits."

So he sneaked up on those three little puppies and took their puppy-biscuit lunch.

Poor little puppies!

They were really very hungry. And they felt very sad.

Just then, who should appear but the fourth little puppy, that Scamp of a puppy, tugging his great big bone!

"Hi, folks," he said. "Look what I found. How about joining me?"

So they ate the big, juicy bone for lunch. And they all had a fine time.

When picnic time was over, those three pretty puppies all went happily home.

And the fourth little puppy, that Scamp of a puppy, walked proudly at the head of the line.

UNCLE REMUS

PICTURES BY BOB GRANT FOR THE WALT DISNEY STUDIO

ADAPTED FROM THE CHARACTERS AND BACKGROUNDS CREATED FOR

WALT DISNEY'S "SONG OF THE SOUTH"

RETOLD BY MARION PALMER

FROM THE ORIGINAL "UNCLE REMUS" STORIES

BY JOEL CHANDLER HARRIS

Brer Rabbit's Laughing Place

WAY DOWN DEEP in de brier-patch is de home of Brer Rabbit. He is a smart feller, but sometimes he get on de nerves of Brer Bear and Brer Fox.

One night dey catch him and tie him up, to make him into stew.

But Brer Rabbit only laugh at Brer Bear and Brer Fox. "Too bad," he say.

"What you mean?" ask Brer Fox.

"I was goin' to show you my secret laughing place in a hollow tree," say Brer Rabbit. "Make me feel like laughin' just to think of it."

"Can't you tell us which tree?" dey ask.

"I can't tell you where 'tis," say Brer Rabbit. "I got to show you. But you got me all tied up.

If you'd set me free, I'd take you dere right now."

Brer Fox and Brer Bear consider more.

At last dey give in. Oh, dey keep a rope on Brer Rabbit, good and tight. Den dey start off, an Brer Rabbit lead de way right up to a hollow oak.

"Dere 'tis!" he yell. "Dere's my laughing place." So Brer Fox and Brer Bear peek in.

Zippety-zim, out come a swarm of bees, an dey chase Brer Fox and Brer Bear a-howling through de woods.

Brer Rabbit, he laugh till he almost choke. "Dat's my laughing place!" he sing out.

So Brer Fox and Brer Bear go on home, mos' unhappy, and dream of trappin' Brer Rabbit again.

Brer Fox and de Rabbit Trap

I'M TIRED OF STAYIN' at home," said Brer Rabbit one day. "I'm goin' away . . . far, far away . . . an I'm goin' to have some fun."

Wid dat, Brer Rabbit walk outer his house. *Blim!* He slam de door. He pick up his hammer. *Blam!* He nail de door up tight. Den off he trot, *lippity-clippity*, down de road.

Brer Rabbit whistle an sing; he feel good.

Well suh, he trot an he trot, an purty soon he trot by a big high fence, wid a field of corn a-growin' on de other side.

"Hmmm," say Brer Rabbit. "Dat corn is Brer Fox's corn. It sure look deelicious." He smack his lips. "It look so deelicious dat I just got to steal a teenchy little taste." He tiptoe to de fence an start to crawl through.

Whrrpp! . . . Somethin' grab round his stummock. *Whoop!* . . . Up in de air whiz Brer Rabbit, swingin' on a rope from de end of a tree branch! "Oh!" he cry. "Dat nasty Brer Fox has ketched me in his trap!"

Just den he see Brer Bear come along. "I'll make dat stupid Bear get me outer dis trap," he say.

"Howdy-do, Brer Bear!" say Brer Rabbit. "I'm doin' dollar-a-minute work. I'm skeering crows away. Dat's more dan you could do."

"I could do it as good as you could do."

"Oh, I couldn't give up dis job," say Brer Rabbit.

Brer Fox, he look out from his hidin' place in de tree trunk.

An what do he see but Brer Rabbit, swingin' over de corn field, ketched in his trap!

He start out for dere, mighty fast.

But Brer Rabbit see him comin'. He know he got to hurry an get outer dat trap real quick.

"Poor Brer Bear!" he say, shakin' his head very sad. "If your pockets ain't stuffed wid big silver dollars, how you goin' to buy your fambly dere Christmas presents? How you goin' to buy de turkey? How you goin' to buy mince pie?"

Now Brer Bear mighty worried. "Dat's right, Brer Rabbit. I got to make money fast! I wish I could do dis dollar-a-minute skeer-crow work!"

"Den pull me down!" say Brer Rabbit. "Pull me down, an we'll change places!"

An dat's just what dey did. By de time Brer Fox get dere, Brer Bear wuz swingin' in de air from de tree branch, an Brer Rabbit wuz down—way cross de field, fillin' up his sack wid sweet, deelicious corn.

Brer Fox so mad he trimble an shake. "What *you* doin' up dere, Brer Bear?" he yell.

"Me?...I'm doin' dollar-a-minute work. Yassir," say Brer Bear, "I'm makin' a dollar-a-minute skeerin' de crows away."

"You *not* makin' a dollar-a-minute! You just makin' a fool of yourself! You let dat sassy Brer Rabbit get away!"

An just den dey hear Brer Rabbit laughin'.

"Toodle-do!" he call from across de field. "Dat's de most fun I ever had!" Wid dat, he grab up his sack full of corn, an away he gallop home.

De Tar Baby

ONE DAY BRER FOX an Brer Bear wuz sittin' round in de woods, an Brer Fox say, all to once, "I'm goin' to make a new sort of trap dat's sure to git Brer Rabbit!"

So he get some tar an set to work. He make him a Tar Baby and dress it in Brer Bear's clothes.

Dey took de Tar Baby, and dey sot him down by de side of de road. Den Brer Fox and Brer Bear, dey hid until Brer Rabbit comes along an spies de Tar Baby. "Howdy-do!" sing out Brer Rabbit.

Of course, de Tar Baby, he say nothin'. Brer Rabbit wait. Den he say, louder dan before, "Ain't you goin' to be perlite an say Howdy-do?"

De Tar Baby, he say nothin'. Now Brer Rabbit get mad. He draw back his fist, an *blip!* he hit de Tar Baby smack in de nose. But Brer Rabbit's fist stuck in de tar.

"Let go my fist!" he holler, an he draw back his other fist, an *blip!* again he hit de Tar Baby. But dis fist stuck, too.

Well suh, Brer Rabbit kicked dat Tar Baby wif both behind feet. Den he ram him wid his head. By now, Brer Rabbit so stuck in de tar, he can't scarcely move at all.

Now Brer Fox and Brer Bear come outer de bushes. Dey dance round an round Brer Rabbit, laughin' an chucklin'.

"Brer Rabbit," say Brer Fox, "you been bossin' other folks round fer a long time. Now I'm de boss, an I'm goin' to roast you."

Brer Rabbit, he skeered, but he think he know how to get out of dis trouble.

"Roast me just ez hot ez you please," say Brer Rabbit, "but please, *please* don't fling me in dat brier-patch!"

"Hold on, Brer Fox," say Brer Bear. "It's goin' to be a lot of trouble to roast Brer Rabbit. First, we got to build a big, hot fire." "Yes . . . dat's so," say Brer Fox. "Well, Brer Rabbit, I guess de best way is to skin you. Come on, Brer Bear, let's get started."

"Skin me," say Brer Rabbit, "pull out my ears, snatch off my legs, an chop off my tail, but please, *please*, PLEASE, Brer Fox an Brer Bear, don't fling me in dat brier-patch!"

Now Brer Bear sorter grumble. "Ah . . . pooh! It ain't goin' to be much fun to skin Brer Rabbit, 'cause he ain't skeered of bein' skinned."

"But he sure is skeered of dat brier-patch!" say Brer Fox. "An dat's just where he's goin' to go!"

Wid dat, he yank Brer Rabbit off de Tar Baby, and he fling him, *kerplunk!* . . . right into de brier-patch!

Well suh, dere wuz a flutter where Brer Rabbit landed, den *"Ooo! Oow! Ouch!"* He screech an he squall. Den after a while, dere is only a weak whisper from Brer Rabbit.

Brer Fox and Brer Bear, dey listen. Den dey laff an shake hands. "We got him! Brer Rabbit is dead!"

But right den, dey hear a scufflin' way at de other end of de brier-patch. An lo an behold, who do dey see scramblin' out but Brer Rabbit hisself, whistlin' an singin', an combin' de tar outer his mustarshes wid a piece of de brier-bush!

"Born an bred in de brier-patch, dat's me," laugh Brer Rabbit. "Told you not to fling me dere. In all de world dat's de place I love best!"

An *lippity clip*, he hop away.

So up an down dat countryside, Brer Fox an Brer Bear chase Brer Rabbit still. Maybe some day dey catch him. You reckon dey will?

MICKEY MOUSE'S PICNIC

STORY BY JANE WERNER

$\mathcal{M}$ickey Mouse sang:

"What a beautiful day for a picnic,
What a picnical day for a lark!
In the happiest way,
We will frolic all day
And we won't get back home until dark!"

Mickey was feeling very happy as he skipped up the walk to Minnie Mouse's house. "Ready Minnie?" he called.

Pluto and Goofy and Daisy Duck and Clarabelle Cow were waiting in Mickey's car.

"Ready!" smiled Minnie. Mickey peeked inside the lunch basket. Minnie had packed huge peanut butter and jelly sandwiches and cold meat sandwiches and deviled eggs and potato salad, radishes, and onions and frosty pink lemonade and a great big chocolate cake!

"Let's go!" said Mickey. And he picked up the basket and led Minnie out to the car.

"It seems strange to go on a picnic without Donald Duck," said Mickey as they drove away.

"Yes, but there is always trouble when Donald is along," said the others.

When they were far down the road, none of them saw a figure come out from hiding and jump up and down in rage! It was Donald Duck!

"What a beautiful day for a picnic,
What a picnical day for a lark!"

everyone sang as Mickey Mouse drove merrily down the road to the picnic grounds.

And it did start out to be a perfect day. First they went for a walk along the riverbank. They found a grassy spot beneath a tall shade tree. And they left Minnie's lunch basket there.

Then everyone went swimming in the old swimming hole. And how good that fresh, cool

water felt! They swam and floated and played around and had a wonderful time.

"I'm hungry enough to eat that whole basketful of lunch myself," Mickey said after a while.

"We'll see that you don't, Mickey!" Minnie laughed. "But it is time to eat, I guess."

So they all scrambled out of the water and hurried off to dress.

"Say!" Goofy cried. "Look at this, will you!"

Goofy was holding up his pants. The legs were tied into knots. So were his shirt sleeves. And Mickey's were, too.

"Well, I never!" said Clarabelle Cow.

"Some mischief-maker must be around," Mickey said, with a shake of his head.

But Minnie had a worse thought than that.

"The lunch!" she cried. And she ran up the bank to the shade of that big old tree.

The lunch basket was gone!

"Oh!" groaned everyone. "Not the lunch!"

"Hurry and get into your clothes, everybody!" Mickey cried. "We'll soon find out about this."

They struggled to undo the knots in their clothes. Then they dressed in a flash and were off on the hunt.

All through the woods they hunted, under every bush and trailing vine. But not a sign of that lunch basket did they see.

At last they came out on the road again, near where they had left Mickey's car. They were hot and tired and hungry and cross.

And it was then that they met Donald Duck, walking along the road all by himself. He had a fishing pole over one shoulder. And a bundle hung from the end of the fishing pole.

Donald was whistling as he walked along, and he looked very pleased with himself.

"Well, hello, hello, hello!" he cried. "Imagine meeting you folks out here. I just came from some fishing myself. Got tired of spending a lonely day at home."

"Oh-er-yes," said Mickey. He felt bad because they had left Donald behind.

"Where are you folks going?" Donald asked.

"We are hunting for our lunch," Mickey said.

"For lunch?" said Donald. "Why, I have enough for us all in my bundle here. I will be glad to share it with my friends."

Now everyone felt guilty. But they were hungry, so they said thank you, they would like to eat with Donald.

Under the same big shady tree, Donald opened his bundle.

The lunch was delicious. There were peanut butter and jelly sandwiches and cold meat sandwiches and deviled eggs and potato salad, radishes, and onions and pink lemonade and a great big chocolate cake!

A strange look came into Mickey and Minnie Mouse's eyes as they saw that picnic lunch. But they did not say a word.

So they all sat down and ate and ate.

"This is delicious, Donald," said Clarabelle Cow.

"And it is nice of you, too, Donald," Daisy Duck added, "to share it with us."

"Sure is," said Goofy, reaching for another sandwich.

"Yes," Mickey admitted, "I guess we misjudged you, Donald, old boy."

"Humph!" said Minnie Mouse. Then she turned to Donald with her sweetest smile.

"Did you bring a knife for cutting the chocolate cake, Donald?" she asked.

"Er—ah, I had one somewhere," Donald said. He looked all around. But he could not find it.

"I fastened a knife to the bottom of my cake pan with paper tape," Minnie said.

Mickey leaned over and looked at the bottom of the cake pan. And there, sure enough, was a knife, fastened to the bottom of the pan with paper tape. On the knife handle were the letters M. M.

"Well!" said Minnie.

"Why, Donald!" cried Daisy Duck.

"So that's where our lunch disappeared to," cried Mickey Mouse.

Donald dropped his eyes. "I'm sorry, honest I am," he said. "I won't ever do it again."

"Where is my lunch basket?" Minnie asked.

"In Mickey's car," Donald admitted.

Mickey had to laugh. "Well," he said as he cut the cake, "we've all learned a lesson, I think. Donald won't snatch lunch baskets anymore. And we know it's better to bring Donald on a picnic."

Everyone had to laugh then. And they all piled back into Mickey's car. They made room for Donald to sit in the empty lunch basket.

Then away they went toward town, singing:

"We will frolic all day
In the happiest way,
And we won't get back home until dark!"

DONALD DUCK
and the Christmas Carol

BY ANNIE NORTH BEDFORD

ADAPTED BY NORMAN McGARY

"*Deck the halls with boughs of holly!*" sang Donald Duck and his nephews.

It was the day before Christmas. They had finished their Chrismas shopping. They were busy trimming their Christmas tree when the doorbell rang.

"Merry Christmas, Merry Christmas!" cried Huey, Louie, and Dewey as they ran to open the door.

"Christmas is a waste of time and money," snapped Uncle Scrooge. "I came to see if you'd drive me out to my farm to bury these sacks of money I've saved up this year.

"You have no money saved up, I'll wager, after buying these fool presents. And it's clear to see you're set on wasting your time, too. So—Bah! Humbug! And good-bye to you!"

Out stamped Uncle Scrooge with his money

"Bah!" said Uncle Scrooge, shaking the snow from his coat as he stamped into the house. "Christmas? Humbug!"

"Christmas, humbug? Why, Uncle Scrooge! How can you say such a thing?" cried Huey, Louie, and Dewey Duck.

sacks. And off he went into the swirling snow.

"Wait, Uncle Scrooge!" called Donald.

"Merry Christmas, Uncle Scrooge," called Huey, Louie, and Dewey.

But Uncle Scrooge just grunted and shook his cane at the jolly crowds of Christmas shoppers.

77

"He will?" said the boys. "Say, why don't we—" and they turned back to their jolly Christmas tree.

Donald was right. Uncle Scrooge stamped home through the snow, all the way across town to his big old empty mansion.

He locked the door behind him. He drew all the curtains and shades.

Then he stamped up the stairs to his cold, dark room. And he propped himself up in bed with a book and a candle to read by.

"Christmas—humbug," he muttered to himself. "I don't care for anyone. And nobody cares for me. That's the way, if I had my say, that everyone would be!"

"Old skinflint!" cried Donald. "Trying to spoil our Christmas just because he won't have one of his own."

"Poor Uncle Scrooge! No Christmas at all! What will he do, Uncle Donald?" asked the boys.

"He'll go home and lock the door and draw the curtains and sit all alone in his dark, cold house, feeling sorry for himself," said Donald Duck.

As the candle sputtered and shadows danced on the walls, Uncle Scrooge's head drooped over his book. He was almost asleep when a knock sounded at his door. In walked a figure dressed all in white, with a holly wreath on its head.

In his hands he carried a big black book.

"Who—who are you?" asked Uncle Scrooge.

"I am the spirit of Christmas Past," said the figure. "Do you remember the fun that you used to have at Christmastime?"

And, putting an old snapshot album into Scrooge's hands, the figure slipped out the door. Uncle Scrooge turned the pages. "Why, here's Daisy" he cried. "With the doll I gave her one year.

"And little Donald on his rocking horse! My, what fun we used to have! I wish—"

Uncle Scrooge was so busy with the snapshots that he did not hear the door open again. A second figure slipped into his room. This one was dressed in red.

"I am the spirit of Christmas Present," said the figure. "Listen to the fun others have at Christmastime—"

And outside the door Scrooge could hear happy voices singing,

"Deck the halls with boughs of holly
Fa la la la la la la la la,
'Tis the season to be jolly,
Fa la la la la la la la la!"

"Bah—" Uncle Scrooge began. But he could not finish. Something caught in his throat. When he looked up again, a third figure was standing beside his bed.

"I am the Spirit of Christmas Yet to Come," said this figure, who was dressed in black. "If you do not mend your ways, you will never have a happy Christmas again."

"But what can I do?" cried Uncle Scrooge.

"Follow me!" said the figure. And Uncle Scrooge scrambled out of bed and followed him out of the gloomy room and down the long, dark stairs.

The figure turned toward the living-room door.

"There's nothing in there but dust," said Uncle Scrooge. But he followed along anyway.

"Merry Christmas, Uncle Scrooge!" cried Daisy and Donald and the nephews, waiting in the living room.

There stood a beautiful Christmas tree. Around it was heaped the biggest pile of presents Uncle Scrooge had ever seen. And some of them were for him!

"When we finish opening presents," said Uncle Scrooge after a while, "let's take my sacks of money and give some to everyone we see who doesn't look as if he's having as merry a Christmas as ours.

"For always remember this, boys! Christmas is the best day of all!"

PINOCCHIO

ADAPTED BY CAMPBELL GRANT

FROM THE WALT DISNEY MOTION PICTURE "PINOCCHIO"

Based on the Story by Collodi

KINDLY OLD GEPPETTO stood at his workbench and carved on a puppet that looked just like a real boy. He sang as he worked, and Little Figaro, his cat, played with the chips as they fell from his knife. Jiminy Cricket chirped merrily on the hearth, and the goldfish, Cleo, swam around and around in her bowl.

"There," said Geppetto, as he held up the puppet, "you're finished."

He held the strings and danced the little wooden boy across the floor.

"How I wish you were a real, live boy!" he said. "What fun we would have, you and Figaro and Cleo and I!"

"What about me?" asked a small voice. "Couldn't I have fun, too?"

"Ho, Jiminy Cricket! Of course you could have fun, too," laughed Geppetto. "You could go everywhere with him to keep him out of trouble. What shall we call him . . . Pinocchio . . . little, wooden-headed Pinocchio?"

"A dandy name, Pinocchio!" cried Jiminy Cricket. He jumped from the floor to the workbench. "A dandy name!"

At that moment all the clocks in the house started to strike. Old Geppetto looked up.

"It's nine o'clock," he said. "Time for sleep."

He placed Pinocchio on the workbench, tumbled Figaro into the big bed, and blew a kiss to Cleo in her bowl. He opened the window, and the light of the Evening Star streamed into the room.

"Star light, star bright . . . ," he said softly. "I wish Pinocchio were a real, live boy!"

He looked once more at the merry little puppet and then settled down in his bed. In a moment he was snoring.

Only Jiminy Cricket was still awake. He was unhappy, thinking Old Geppetto would never have his wish. Suddenly he heard strange, sweet music. The Evening Star sailed down through the sky and into Geppetto's window. The cottage was filled with dazzling light, and there stood a lovely fairy dressed all in blue.

"It's the Blue Fairy!" whispered Jiminy Cricket. "Geppetto will get his wish this time, or my name isn't Jiminy Cricket!"

The Blue Fairy flew to the workbench where little wooden Pinocchio sat, and said:

"*Awake, Pinocchio, and live!*
To you the gift of life I give.
Be good, and bring Geppetto joy,
And grow to be a real, live boy."

You can imagine Geppetto's surprise the next morning, when he found Pinocchio running around!

"I'm dreaming! You can't be alive! You're still made of wood!" said the astonished old man.

"But if I'm brave and good, I'll be a real, live boy someday," said Pinocchio joyfully.

At last Geppetto said, "Now, Pinocchio, it's time for all good boys to go to school." And Pinocchio started out.

"Pinoke!" Jiminy Cricket called. "Wait for me!"

But although the Blue Fairy had told Pinocchio that Jiminy Cricket was to be his friend and conscience, Pinocchio did not hear the voice of his little friend.

Suddenly, something tripped Pinocchio. It was a cane, thrust between his flying feet by the sly old fox, J. Worthington Foulfellow.

Foulfellow helped Pinocchio to his feet and winked at his partner Gideon, the bad cat.

"Ha ha, Pinocchio," began Foulfellow, "you were going a little too fast! A little too fast, and in the *wrong* direction. Now I have a plan for you. Come. . . ."

"But I'm on my way to school," said Pinocchio.

"To school? Nonsense!" said Foulfellow. "I have a much better plan—a trip to Pleasure Island!"

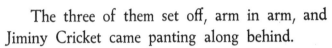

The two villains told Pinocchio about Pleasure Island, with its lollypop trees, and ice-cream mountains, and its Mayor who let the boys do whatever they wanted. And the little wooden-headed puppet forgot all about Geppetto and the happy little workshop. He decided to go to Pleasure Island right away.

The three of them set off, arm in arm, and Jiminy Cricket came panting along behind.

Soon they came to a great coach. The two scoundrels took from the wicked-looking coachman a large bag of gold. They had sold Pinocchio!

Jiminy was frightened, but he hopped bravely aboard just as the coach drove off.

The coach was pulled by six sad-looking little donkeys. It was filled with boys of all sizes and ages, a noisy, rowdy lot. Pinocchio made friends with the leader, a loud boy named Lampwick. But Jiminy sadly hid in a corner.

Pleasure Island was wonderful—just as Foulfellow had said. And when Jiminy Cricket tried

to get Pinocchio to go home, Pinocchio turned his back on his tiny friend.

"I'll go back after awhile," he said. "Right now, I want some fun!"

"You bet!" yelled Lampwick. "Come on!"

Every day they played. They ate candy and ice cream and cake and more candy. They broke windows, and threw mud, and carved up furniture.

"Good," said the Mayor. "Go to it, boys!"

"Fine," cried the Coachman. "They're almost ready!"

"Pinocchio!" begged Jiminy Cricket. "Please come with me!"

"Who's the goody-goody?" sneered Lampwick.

"Yah," Pinocchio said, "go away, Cricket! I'm tired of you!"

He looked at Lampwick for approval. Right before his eyes, Lampwick's ears became long and fuzzy . . . then he grew a tail . . . and then, in a twinkling of an eye, Lampwick turned into a little donkey!

The Coachman came running and put a rope around Lampwick's neck.

"Aha!" he cried, "another donkey to sell to the man who runs the salt mines!"

He reached for Pinocchio, because Pinocchio was growing donkey ears and a donkey tail, too. But Jiminy Cricket shouted, "Run, Pinocchio! Come on!"

And *this* time Pinocchio ran with Jiminy Cricket. They ran to the edge of the island and dived into the water and swam away from that terrible place.

Hours later, wet and tired, they came to Geppetto's cottage. But no one was there. Old Geppetto had taken Figaro and Cleo and gone to search for Pinocchio.

Poor Pinocchio! "It's all my fault," he told Jiminy Cricket. "Will I ever find my father again?"

"I don't know," said Jiminy. "It might be a dangerous task."

"I don't mind," declared Pinocchio. "It's my job to find him, even if it is dangerous."

So away went Pinocchio, with Jiminy beside him. And what adventures they did have!

They even chased a whale to the bottom of the sea. And the Blue Fairy watched them all the way. She was watching when they found Geppetto at last, and led him safely home.

It was only then that Geppetto noticed Pinocchio's donkey ears.

"I'm sorry, Father," Pinocchio said humbly. "But I do know better now."

Suddenly the Evening Star brightened the room, and the Blue Fairy appeared.

"You have learned your lesson well, Pinocchio," she said. And as her magic wand touched him, Pinocchio felt himself turn into a real boy!

"Father!" he cried, "I'm a real boy at last!"

Geppetto hugged him and laughed and cried for joy. And as for Jiminy Cricket, the Fairy gave him a badge of gold. And on the badge it said:

Awarded to a Good Conscience
who helped to make
a real boy out of a Wooden Head.

THE ARISTOCATS

AUTHORIZED EDITION

Based on the popular
motion picture

In Madame Bonfamille's fine home in Paris, all was peaceful. Well, almost. . . .

"Me first!" Kitten Marie shouted. "I'm a lady!"

"Ha! You're not a lady," said her brother Toulouse.

"You're just a sister," said Berlioz.

"I'll show you!" Marie shouted.

Marie started after her brothers. A chase began that brought giggles and then tears, as Marie's tail somehow arrived in Berlioz's mouth.

"Children!" said Duchess, their mother.

"I was just practicing my biting, Mamma," said Berlioz.

"Aristocats do not bite," said Duchess. "Come, let's practice being ladies and gentlemen."

Soon all was peaceful again—but not for long. Out in the kitchen, someone was planning to do something bad to the Aristocats.

Edgar the butler had heard Madame say, "I'm leaving my fortune to my dear cats. Edgar may have what's left when they're gone."

Edgar had thought, "Four cats. Nine lives each. Four times nine is . . . is . . . too long. They'll outlive me, unless. . . ."

And, right then and there, Edgar planned a way to make the Aristocats disappear.

"Come, kitties," he called. "Come taste this delicious *crème de la Edgar.*"

It *was* delicious. Their friend Roquefort the mouse thought so, too. But . . . everyone who drank it fell asleep!

And the Aristocats slept *so* soundly that they didn't know they left home in a basket on Edgar's motorcycle. They didn't know that Edgar was chased by dogs, and that the basket fell off and landed under a bridge.

They didn't know they were alone, far out in the country, until a storm broke and they woke up.

"Mamma!" Marie called out. "I'm afraid! Where are we?"

"I don't know, darling. I . . . I. . . . Let's just try to sleep until morning."

But Duchess couldn't sleep. All she could do was worry.

Then she heard a rough voice singing, "I'm O'Malley the Alley Cat. Helpin' ladies is my—"

"Oh, Mr. O'Malley, can you help me?" Duchess called. "I'm in great trouble. I'm lost."

O'Malley bowed. "Yer ladyship, I'll fly you off on my magic carpet for two."

Berlioz popped up. So did Toulouse. And Marie. "What magic carpet?" they asked.

"Uh . . . er . . ." O'Malley stammered. Then he grinned "Look, I said magic carpet for two, but it can be a magic carpet for *five* also." He made an X on the road. "It'll stop for passengers right here. Watch!"

They watched. Soon something came down the road. O'Malley made himself big and scary-

looking and jumped out in front of it. The something stopped right on the X.

"All aboard!" said O'Malley. "One magic carpet, ready to go."

"Aw, it's just a truck," said Berlioz.

"Shh!" said Duchess. Then she smiled at O'Malley. "It's a lovely magic carpet. Is it going to Paris?" she asked.

"It's goin' somewhere," said O'Malley, helping her on.

But soon the driver of the magic carpet saw that he had passengers. He stopped with a jerk. He shouted terrible things, and when he threw a heavy wrench at his passengers, they jumped to safety.

"What an awful man!" said Duchess. "I wish we were home."

"Humans are like that," said O'Malley.

"Oh, no, Mr. O'Malley," said Duchess. "*My* humans aren't like that."

"Hmm!" said OMalley. "Then how did you get here? Somebody doesn't like you."

Duchess thought about that as they began the long walk back to Paris.

Finally they arrived in the city, so tired they could hardly take a step.

"We'll stop and rest at my peaceful pad," O'Malley said.

But the peaceful pad was bouncing with sound. "Oh . . . uh . . . some friends have stopped by," O'Malley explained. "We'll go somewhere—"

"I'd like to meet your friends, Mr. O'Malley," said Duchess.

So O'Malley introduced all his swinging musician friends. What fun it was! They played for the four Aristocats, and Duchess sang for them.

Then, after the children were tucked in, Duchess and O'Mally talked.

"Your friends are delightful," said Duchess.

"How about sharin' them with me?" asked Mr. O'Malley. "I mean, how about stayin' here with me? Like forever."

Marie heard him. She whispered, "Oh, Mr. O'Malley's going to be our father . . . maybe."

"Great!" said Toulouse.

"Shhh!" said Marie. "Listen!"

"Oh, if only I could" said Duchess. "But I can never leave Madame."

"She's lucky," said O'Malley. "I never felt that way about a human, and no human ever felt that way about me." He sighed. "But . . . well, I'll take you home."

The next day, O'Malley watched as Edgar opened the door for the Aristocats.

"Now," Edgar said, "you're going in this trunk to Timbuktu and *never* coming back! Onto the baggage truck you go and away forever." He opened the door.

But suddenly alley cats were everywhere. Two unlocked the trunk and let out the Aristocats.

And some, with a little help, put Edgar inside. Now someone else was on his way to Timbuktu!

And there were some happy cats who were very glad to stay home. Listen! You can hear a rough voice, and a lovely soft voice, and three little voices singing. . . .

"We're Mr. and Mrs. O'Malley. We're the *five* Aristocats."

"Oh!" said Edgar. "You're back! I mean . . . uh, how *nice* to see you back!"

"Looks like they don't need me anymore," said O'Malley. He turned away sadly.

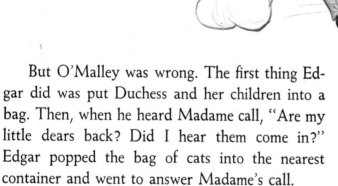

But O'Malley was wrong. The first thing Edgar did was put Duchess and her children into a bag. Then, when he heard Madame call, "Are my little dears back? Did I hear them come in?" Edgar popped the bag of cats into the nearest container and went to answer Madame's call.

The four Aristocats were stiff with fear. What would happen to them now? Then Duchess remembered Roquefort the mouse. "Get O'Malley!" she called. She told him how to find her friend. "Hurry!"

Roquefort ran out, just as Edgar came back in with a trunk.

THE Jungle Book

ADAPTED FROM THE MOWGLI STORIES BY RUDYARD KIPLING

TOLD BY ANNIE NORTH BEDFORD

MANY STRANGE legends are told of the jungles of far-off India. They speak of Bagheera the black panther, of Baloo the bear. They tell of Kaa the sly python, and of the Lord of the Jungle, the great tiger, Shere Khan. But of all the legends none is so strange as the story of a small boy named Mowgli.

The story began when a child, left all alone in the jungle, was found by Bagheera the panther. He could not give the small, helpless "man-cub" care and nourishment, so Bagheera took him to the den of a wolf family with young cubs of their own.

That is how it happened that Mowgli, as the man-cub came to be called, was raised among the wolves. All the jungle folk were his friends.

Bagheera took Mowgli on long walks and taught him jungle lore.

Baloo, the bumbling bear, played games with Mowgli and taught him to live a life of ease. There were coconuts for the cracking, bananas for the peeling, sweet and juicy pawpaws to pick from jungle trees.

Hathi, the proud old leader of the elephant herd, tried to train young Mowgli in military drill as he led his troop trumpeting down the jungle trails.

Sly old Kaa the python would have loved to squeeze Mowgli tight in his coils. But Mowgli's friends warned him against Kaa.

It was Shere Khan the tiger who was the real danger to Mowgli. That was because Shere Khan, like all tigers, had a hatred of man.

Ten times the season of rains had come to the jungle where Mowgli made his home with the wolf family. Then Shere Khan returned to the wolves' hunting grounds.

The wolf pack met at Council Rock when next the moon was full.

So it was arranged, and when the greenish light of the jungle morning slipped through the leaves, Bagheera and Mowgli set out.

All day they walked, and when night fell they slept on a high branch of a giant banyan tree. All this seemed like an adventure to Mowgli. But when he learned that he was to leave the jungle, he was horrified.

"No!" cried Mowgli. "The jungle is my home. I can take care of myself. I will stay!"

He slipped down a length of trailing vine and rudely ran away.

For a while Mowgli marched with Hathi and the elephants. But he soon tired of that.

Then he found Baloo bathing in a jungle pool. Mowgli joined him for a dip.

Suddenly down swooped the monkey folk, the noisy, foolish *Bandar-log*. They had snatched Mowgli from the pool before Baloo knew what was happening.

"As you know," said Akela, the leader of the pack, "Shere Khan the tiger has returned. If he learns that our pack is harboring a man-cub, danger will be doubled for all our families. Are we agreed that the man-cub must go?"

Out from the shadows stepped Bagheera the panther.

"I brought the man-cub to the pack," he said. "It is my duty to see him safely out of the jungle. I know a man-village not far away where he will be well cared for."

They tossed him through the air from hand to hand, and swung him away through the trees.

Off in the jungle, Bagheera heard Mowgli's cry and came with a leap and a bound.

"The monkeys have stolen Mowgli away!" gasped Baloo.

Off raced Bagheera and Baloo to the ruined city where the monkeys made their home.

They found Mowgli a prisoner of the monkey king.

"Teach me the secret of fire," the monkey king ordered Mowgli. "The magic of fire will frighten even Shere Khan. With it I shall be the equal of men. Until I know the secret, you are my prisoner."

It took quite a fight for Bagheera and Baloo to rescue Mowgli that time!

"Now you see," they told him, "why you must go to the man-village to be safe."

But alas, that foolish boy would not understand. He kicked up his heels and ran away again.

This time his wanderings led him to where Shere Khan lay waiting in the high grass, smiling a hungry smile.

When Mowgli caught sight of the tiger, Shere Khan asked, "Well, man-cub, aren't you going to run?"

But Mowgli did not have the wisdom to be afraid. "Why should I run?" he asked, staring Shere Khan in the eye as the tiger gathered himself for a spring. "I'm not afraid of you."

"That foolish boy!" growled Bagheera, who had crept close just in time to hear Mowgli.

Both Bagheera and Baloo flung themselves upon the Lord of the Jungle, to save Mowgli once more. They were brave and strong, but the tiger was mighty of tooth and claw.

There was a flash of lightning and a dead tree nearby caught fire. Mowgli snatched a burning branch and waved it in Shere Khan's face. The tiger, terrified, ran away. Mowgli was very pleased with himself as he strutted between the two weary warriors, Bagheera and Baloo.

Suddenly Mowgli stopped. From ahead came a sound that was strange to him. He peeked through the brush. It was the song of a village girl who had come to fill her water jar.

As he listened to the soft notes of her song, Mowgli felt strange inside. He felt that he must follow her. Mowgli crept up the path to the village, following the girl and her song.

Baloo and Bagheera watched the small figure as long as it could be seen. When Mowgli vanished inside the village gate, Bagheera sighed a deep sigh. "It is just as it should be, Baloo," he said. "Our Mowgli is safe in the man-village at last. He's with his own people now. He has found his true home."